The Secret of KUALOA

A sequel to
The Microchip Caper

BY ROBERT GRAHAM

Illustrations by Sharon Alshams

ISLAND HERITAGE

THE SECRET OF KUALOA

Written by Robert Graham

Illustrated by Sharon Alshams

Published by

ISLAND HERITAGE
P U B L I S H I N G

99-880 IWAENA STREET
AIEA, HAWAII 96701
(808) 487-7299
EMAIL: HAWAII4U@ISLANDHERITAGE.COM

ISBN NO. 089610-323-4
First Edition, First Printing – 1999

Dedicated To
Children Who Love Books,
Especially
Dionne, Donna, and Merlin

Contents

CHAPTER I
A Sudden Wind

The moon, just past its full phase, shone bright as a silver dollar against a dark sky. Pin pricks of stars decorated the heavens, while beneath a scattering of damp, misty clouds, *Adventurer* sailed its way through the gently heaving ocean. The summer breezes pushed the boat onward around the Hawaiian island of Oʻahu.

"We're coming around Kualoa," Kai called. "Only a few more miles until we anchor."

"Yes, we're almost there," Mr. Parkson nodded to his son's friend. He turned off the flashlight he had been using to check the navigation chart. They had made good time on the short sail from Honolulu.

The boat with its three passengers cut through the water, gliding past Kualoa. In the darkness, that mountainous ridge seemed to block their way, as if it wanted to reach out across the water to grab them and hold them fast. A sudden, chill wind whistled down from the mountain. It was gone as fast as it had come.

"Chicken skin! Did you feel that?" shouted Kai.

Mr. Parkson, trying to keep the boat on its course, in spite of a wind that had suddenly shifted and waves

that were knocking them toward shore, was too busy to respond.

"You mean that breeze?" said thirteen-year-old Todd Parkson from the other side of the deck.

"Yeah," Kai replied, moving into the shadows with his friend. "The Hawaiians say *chicken skin* when something freaky like that makes you shiver. They would think that wind came from the ancient gods."

"Oh, come on. You're always saying things like that. Ancient gods . . . no way! You should have been with us when we sailed this boat from San Diego, then you'd be used to little breezes like that. That was nothing," said Todd.

"And you're always saying things like that!" Kai retorted angrily. *"That's just the problem,"* he thought to himself; *"You can't share feelings with strangers."* But he really knew that Todd and his family were no longer strangers after the six months they'd known each other. In fact, they had become close friends.

"What are those lights? Over there on the mountain." Todd pointed to five spots that flickered with a yellow intensity and seemed to be moving down the mountain. The boys stared at the string of lights. Every few seconds one of the lights was temporarily lost to sight, apparently blocked by trees or bushes on the mountainside.

Todd scuttled over to where Kai gazed intently toward the valley. "What is it?" he asked, all the while thinking that it must be hunters after wild pigs or some such thing. Newcomer to the islands though he was, he felt sure that he had already learned enough so that there were no secrets that could be hidden from him.

Kai, because of his Hawaiian upbringing and a lifetime in the islands, didn't feel so confident. In fact, he felt as if something wasn't right. The wind had sent a chill down his back, and now he felt a queasiness in his stomach as he gazed uneasily at the torches which continued to move toward the valley floor.

Then the first light disappeared. They waited for it to reappear, but it didn't. A moment later, the second flickering beam reached the same spot and it, too, disappeared, as did the lights that followed. The mountainside was again clothed only in darkness.

As the boys looked questioningly toward Kualoa, the wind sprang up, but this time it came more forcefully and it came from the mountain. In an instant, the sails, which had been hanging almost slack, were filled with the onrushing air. Still the wind came, and the thirty-five foot boat began to heel over.

Mr. Parkson grasped the wheel, swinging it so that *Adventurer* would turn with the wind and right itself, but for some reason the boat didn't respond. Instead, it heeled farther and farther over.

As *Adventurer* slid over on its side, its wooden timbers creaked, and the sound of tumbling furniture and crashing dishes came from the cabins. The boys grabbed the edge of the deck so they wouldn't slide to the other side. Todd struggled to hold on, wondering if they would capsize.

"Remember the life jackets under the seats," Mr. Parkson shouted as he held onto the wheel. While he worried for the boys, himself, and the boat, he said a quick prayer of thanks that his wife and the girls had stayed behind at Uncle Bob's house.

For a few seconds the boat remained suspended a breath away from capsizing; then as suddenly as it had begun, the wind died. The sails, emptied of air, beat loosely. *Adventurer* fell back, smacking the water as it righted itself. In the sudden quiet a last gust of wind carried what seemed to be the sound of a drum from the mountain to the watchful sailors.

Mr. Parkson swung the wheel and this time the boat responded and headed away from the nearby coral reef against which the waves broke in a booming warning.

"Drums," Kai muttered darkly.

"What? What did you say?" Todd asked.

"Drums. Those were drums I heard just then. Man, I thought we were going to die. I know what that must have been, all those lights, wind, and drums. It could only be one thing."

He paused, taking a deep breath of the cool night air. Looking over his shoulder, he could see the darkened silhouette of Kualoa where a few minutes before there had been those torches.

"It must have been nightmarchers." He said it almost to himself, but Todd heard him.

CHAPTER II

Nightmarchers

When *Adventurer* had righted itself, Mr. Parkson turned the wheel over to Todd and went forward to check for damage. Making his way along the deck, he held tightly to the guide ropes in case another freak wind struck them. He checked the sails, rigging, and lines for any damage.

After a few anxious moments, he decided that all appeared normal, although a complete check would have to wait until morning light. Returning to the stern deck, he looked at the water and the few clouds overhead, then sniffed the air to try and get a sense of the approaching weather. All appeared calm, but that previous wind had given no warning either. He would feel better when they were safely anchored in Kahana Bay. If the wind held, they should be there within the hour, about 5 A.M.

"Kai, what's that you were talking about?" he asked as he stepped into the cockpit and took control of the wheel from Todd.

"The nightmarchers, spirits of old Hawaiians. They're called *ka huaka'i po* in Hawaiian. Those torches must have been them," Kai said.

"Oh, come on. You don't believe that. Ghosts, man? You must be crazy. I didn't see any ghosts or spirits out here, it was only the wind. Right, Dad?" Todd turned to his father for support.

"Well, I suppose so, son," Mr. Parkson said, not sure exactly what the boys had been talking about. "What's this about nightmarchers?"

Kai shook his head, he wasn't sure if he wanted to share his knowledge with two people who probably wouldn't agree with the Hawaiian beliefs. Already Todd had shown that he couldn't accept the idea that things might not be exactly what they first seemed. Kai sighed. He remembered how his grandfather often said that newcomers to the islands didn't believe what Hawaiians knew in their hearts to be true.

Still, the Parksons had become his friends. They were generous and kind, and he felt he could trust them. Besides, he was about to burst with the excitement and fear that he felt from his first actual experience with nightmarchers. He had heard many stories about those spirits of the dead, but had never before *seen* them. "It's kind of hard to explain," he began.

"Go on, tell us what you know," Mr. Parkson urged.

Leaning back against the wooden bench, Kai tried to get comfortable despite the fact that all the vinyl cushions had slipped overboard when the boat had nearly capsized. What were those stories his grandfather had told him? How should he explain the ancient beliefs to these people?

In a quiet voice he began, "In old Hawaii, the high chiefs were buried in secret caves in the mountains.

Their bones would be hidden away with their feather cloaks, images of the gods, and other valuable things. Of course, most of those chiefs went on to a spirit world, but for some reason some of the spirits stayed here. The ones who stayed are called the nightmarchers. On certain nights they reappear."

"What's that have to do with us? We didn't see anybody. There were just those lights, then a big wind," Todd said.

"That's just it. From what my grandfather says, you don't usually see the nightmarchers. Most people just see the torches they carry and sometimes hear the beating of their drums," Kai explained.

"Hmmmm. Drums, you say?" Mr. Parkson questioned. "Wasn't there a sound like drums just before the boat righted itself?"

"That's right," Kai nodded. "That's what made me think of nightmarchers. Those torches on the mountainside could have been them."

"Oh come on. Isn't there a road where those lights were? It was probably cars going down the mountain," Todd said.

Kai snorted with laughter. "Cars! You'll have to see that mountain tomorrow during the day. It's practically straight up, there's no road going up there. And I'll bet the whole thing is riddled with caves where Hawaiians could be buried. It makes sense to me."

Silence fell over the three as they thought about what had been said. For a moment the only sound was of the water sliding against the hull as *Adventurer* sailed onward. Turning from the wheel, Mr. Parkson gazed at the boys whose dark figures were sprawled behind him. He wasn't thinking of the lights on the mountain, but of the wind that had risen and died so suddenly. It had been like nothing he had ever experienced.

"What about that wind? It was strange the way it came up from nowhere," he said.

"I'm not sure about that," Kai said. "But Hawaiians believe that whatever happens in nature has something to do with their gods."

Todd yawned. "There's nothing you could say that will convince me. I'm just glad we weren't all thrown overboard."

An hour later, shortly before dawn, *Adventurer* entered Kahana Bay. Once the anchor had been let out, the boys slipped off to their cabin to sleep. Mr. Parkson tied up loose ropes and gave a last check to the weather conditions which he decided looked fine.

Tomorrow, the rest of the family, along with Kai's sister, would drive out from Honolulu, and they would all be expecting to sail to the island of Kaua'i. But in the cabins everything had been thrown around when the boat had nearly overturned, and that would have to be cleaned up first. The trip might have to be delayed. Mr. Parkson rechecked the anchor, yawned, and went below to sleep.

CHAPTER III

A Surprising Discovery

The next day, in the bright sunlight of early morning, the two boys got off the city bus that had carried them from the bay to Kualoa. Underneath a swinging sign that proclaimed, 'Kualoa Ranch,' Kai unlatched a gate and ushered his friend onto the ranch lands. Horses scampered in all directions as the boys made their way to the stables.

"I don't know why we're doing this," Todd said. "Dad's going to kill me when he wakes up and finds that we left the boat without his permission."

"We're here because you don't believe there are such things as burial caves. I'm going to prove to you that they exist. We're going to borrow two horses and ride up to that mountain we saw from the boat last night. Then you'll see that I'm not kidding or making up things when I talk about Hawaii." Kai stopped, out of breath from his outburst, and surprised at his own anger.

Todd looked around the valley where horses and cattle grazed, his eyes lingered on Kualoa Ridge. It was just like Kai had described it from the boat, it seemed to rise straight up from the valley floor. Clearly there could be no roads going up its steep sides.

"How did I get myself into this?" he wondered. He had no desire to try to get up to where the caves might be, and he didn't want to admit that he knew almost nothing about horseback riding either. He wanted to get back to the boat before his father woke up. "I didn't mean there couldn't be caves," he agreed meekly.

"You did, too!" Kai replied hotly.

"Well, what I meant is," Todd said, trying to compromise, without seeming to back down, "there might be burial caves in these mountains. It's those other things I don't believe in. Those ghosts, or nightmarchers, whatever you called them."

"You're not getting out of it so easily," Kai said. "You'll never believe in nightmarchers unless you see that some of what I say is true. We might not find a burial cave, but at least you'll see there are caves where Hawaiians could have buried their dead."

"Come on," Kai said when he saw a ranch cowboy watching them. "We'll tell him we want to go for a ride, then we'll go up the mountain looking for caves." In a friendly way he put his arm around Todd's shoulder, aware that if he pressured his friend too much, Todd might refuse to go at all.

A while later, they were saddled and riding around the mountain and toward the valley on the other side. The ranch hand's warning rang in their ears, "Don't take any of those trails that lead up the side of the mountain. It's so steep there, the horses could easily stumble."

Todd had meant it when he had nodded his agreement, but Kai had intentions other than following that advice. In fact, what he really planned to do was to try and find the exact spot where the torches had disappeared the night before. That might be where a cave was. But he kept his plan to himself, knowing that Todd would never agree to it.

The horses took them down the trail, away from the beach and highway. On either side, mountainous ridges raised themselves almost straight up from the flat valley floor. Far ahead, a pointed peak stood out alone where the valley came to a head. For all that distance, there were no houses or cars, and the only sound was the wind whistling through the tall grass. It was as if they'd left the noise and bustle of modern life behind.

Farther along, the trail narrowed and wound its way between bushy trees with sharp thorns that brushed against the riders. Todd held tightly to the reins of his gray mare, ignoring the thorns that tore at his pants and worrying instead about falling off the horse or being knocked off by a branch.

Suddenly, Kai galloped ahead. "Yahoo! Isn't this great! What a fantastic, beautiful place."

Todd nodded, although in fact he was too concerned with staying on his horse to appreciate the scenery. To catch up with his friend, he gingerly kicked the horse, but afraid of going too fast, he pulled in on the reins at the same time. The mare snorted at the contradictory signals, shook its head, and trotted forward as Todd bounced from side to side in the saddle. "Maybe we should go back now," he said as he came alongside Kai.

"Are you crazy? We just got started, and we said

we'd keep these horses for three hours. I know what we've got to do. Follow me."

Leaving the main trail, Kai found a path that started up the mountain. The horses climbed slowly, picking their way through the loose boulders and stones that littered the incline.

"Remember what that ranch man said about this kind of trail," Todd warned.

"How we gonna check out the caves if we don't go up?" Kai said in reply.

Nodding glumly, Todd looked out at the view. Already they had climbed high enough so that they could look down on the green valley below. In the distance the sunlight sparkled on the ocean. It was a pretty sight, but he still felt they shouldn't be there.

With a few more minutes of climbing, the trail had become so steep that the horses had to scramble to keep their balance. Barely managing to hang on, Todd was relieved to see Kai get off his horse and signal him to do the same.

The Hawaiian youth scanned the path ahead, not wanting to admit that he couldn't tell if they were still on a trail or following one of the many dried up streams. "We'll have to go on by foot," he announced.

Catching his breath, Todd stepped onto a large rock to look up at the cliffs that lay ahead. He didn't think there was any point in going on, already they had come further than he knew they should have. "I . . . ." he began, then lost his balance, slipped off the rock, and sprawled face down in the dust. The rock rolled toward the horses.

Kai ran to his friend's aid. "Are you OK?"

"I guess so," Todd said.

Behind them, the horses whinnied and the boys turned to see one of them nervously lifting its leg away from the stone that had rolled onto its hoof.

"I sure hope there's nothing wrong with the horse," Kai said, striding toward it. He ran his hand along the animal's leg and then around the hoof, but nothing felt broken, and there were no marks of injury.

Together, the boys pushed the rock a few feet from the horses, and Kai looked around for anything else that might injure the animals. Something on the ground caught his eye.

In the light colored dirt, underneath where the rock had been, was a small, dark stone. Its straight lines had caught his attention, and he picked it up, not suspecting what he had found. Then it hit him, "Look at this, it's a real adze." He rubbed it against his shirt and the stone glowed as if highly polished.

"It's an adze!" he repeated, not believing his luck in finding one. "It was a cutting tool, kind of like a chisel, that the ancient Hawaiian people used. There wasn't any metal in Hawaii before Europeans came, so the Hawaiians had to make stone tools like this. It must be at least 200 years old."

"What will you do with it?" Todd said. He ran his fingers along the stone's smooth edges.

"Keep it for sure. My grandfather has a few of these he found when he was a boy, but they're rare. You usually only see them in museums."

About to slip it into his pocket, he instead put it in

the horse's saddle bag where he wouldn't have to worry about losing it on the hike. Then he took a deep breath. He was more convinced than ever that there was something else to be discovered on this mountain.

Glancing along the ridge, he tried to imagine where the lights had disappeared the night before. It must have been about this height, or maybe a little bit higher. He scrambled up the trail, sure that he was going to find some further treasure. Reluctantly, Todd followed.

CHAPTER IV
The Fall

As the boys climbed higher in the direction where Kai believed the torches had disappeared, the trail became steeper and less clear. To steady himself on the narrow path, Todd held onto the rocks and tried not to gaze downward at the valley far below. One misstep could mean a plunge to his death.

In front of him, Kai moved onward. The youth was impelled by a belief that they were in the area where the torches had been. He had visions of feather capes and statues of ancient gods that might have been buried with the bones of high chiefs. If only they could find a burial cave.

He paused to wipe away the sweat that beaded his forehead and poured into his eyes. Above him, along the cliff, were several spots that might be entrances to caves. Or were they just dark shadows caused by passing clouds? He stepped back to get a better view, then felt his feet begin to slip.

"Help! Help!" he cried as his feet scrambled for surer footing. But the rocks and earth gave way, and he fell backward into the open air.

Todd watched, horrified, as his friend, clawing at the air, disappeared from the ledge. The valley lay far below — a drop of several hundred feet, and for a moment Todd was too stunned to move. He gaped at the spot where Kai had stood. Edging his way cautiously forward, Todd kneeled and dared to look over the side. Perhaps some miracle had placed a large outcropping of rock underneath the ledge and Kai would be there. But it was not to be.

There was no sign of his friend. Instead, Todd looked almost straight down the dizzying height to the ground far below. His head spinning, he drew back, afraid that he, too, might fall, or that a gust of wind would catch him and send him over the side. After a moment of shock he realized that he would have to go back to the horses and find help.

He prayed that somehow Kai would be all right. In fact, wasn't that his voice? He searched the ledge, hoping to see his friend. Could it have been his imagination that Kai had fallen, or perhaps he had been playing some kind of cruel joke. But there was no one else around, and the broken earth at his feet gave clear evidence that the ledge had collapsed.

About to start down the trail, he heard a voice again. This time he was sure that's what it was. He cupped his ears, listened intently, and recognized a feeble cry for help coming from below. Surely it was Kai's voice. Again he leaned over the ledge, but saw only the same view of the valley below. Dangerously, he leaned out further and spied the branches of an old tree that had managed to attach itself to the side of the mountain a few feet directly beneath him.

In that old ʻohiʻa tree, although Todd couldn't see him, lay his friend. As luck would have it, Kai had tumbled from the cliff into the tree's thick branches. Breaking through the top-most limbs, he had grasped at anything to stop his fall. Now he lay where he had come to rest, holding onto the trunk and too frightened to move.

"Kai? Kai?" Todd called from above.

For a moment, Kai ignored Todd's voice and instead concentrated on getting to a small patch of level ground at the tree's base. When he had reached the lowest branches of the tree, he dropped onto the soil. The small patch of grass was cool and moist, and he buried his face in it, thankful that he was alive.

After a moment he looked above him to where Todd must be. A rock ledge stuck out there, so it was impossible to see his friend, but he called anyway. "I'm here!" There was no response, so he called more loudly, "I'm OK!"

Above him, Todd heard and leaned back with relief. His friend was alive! Holding tightly to the ground, he crawled toward the ledge and yelled into the emptiness, "Where are you?"

"I'm right below. It's a little patch of ground. I think you could pull me up with some rope."

"Rope?" Todd looked around, wondering where he could get rope on the side of this lonely mountain. Then he remembered the horses — surely there was rope with them. He would have to find where they had left them, get the rope, and return to this spot all by himself.

He wasn't sure if he would be able to do it, but he would have to try.

The wind swept away half of what the boys yelled to each other, so it took several minutes for Todd to be sure that Kai had understood his plan. Finally, Todd yelled good-bye and got started.

Left alone on the side of the mountain, Kai got to his feet. He had said he was OK, but he wasn't really sure. That fall could have broken a bone. His right side ached, and it hurt to try to stand up straight. Feeling his legs and arms, he decided that he wasn't injured, then he sat wearily on the ground.

He wanted to stretch out and lay down, but the ledge was so small that if he fell asleep, he might roll over and tumble off. It was an impossible situation, so he climbed onto some rocks where he could at least lean against the cliff. Able to stretch his legs out in front of him, he began to relax until he felt a draft on his neck. Where was that air coming from? He turned and pushed away the vines that covered the mountainside behind him. There seemed to be a cave back there, its entrance almost concealed by the rocks and overhanging bushes.

Without thinking, he began to push away the stones that blocked the cave's entrance. Inside that cave he would feel safer; there wouldn't be the danger that he might fall. He rolled a boulder to the side and slid inside. The darkness and coolness of the cave seemed to welcome him, and almost as soon as he stretched out on its rocky floor he was asleep.

CHAPTER V

Inside The Cave

When he woke a short while later, it took Kai a moment
to realize where he was. Then it all came back to him,
the fall, hitting the tree, the cave. Scrambling to his feet,
hoping that Todd had already returned with the rope, he
climbed out of the cave and onto the ledge. But there
was no rope dangling there to rescue him. Dejectedly, he
returned to the cave, wondering if his buddy would be
able to find a way to pull him to safety.

The cool wind that had made him notice the cave's
entrance, again brushed against him. Then it dawned on
him that there had to be a source for that wind. Where
was it coming from? There might be another entrance
to the cave, possibly an escape route.

He gazed with curiosity around the cave's dark
interior, then began to edge his way farther inside, sliding his hands forward to guide him along the rock
walls. After a few steps he was surrounded by total
darkness and he stumbled and knocked against the wall
several times, but the feel of the wind was still there and
he pressed on.

Brushing away spider webs that broke over his

face, he edged himself around the rocks that tried to block his path. Then he came to what seemed to be a solid wall and for a moment he thought he had reached the end of the cave. But as he continued to search, he felt a low, narrow gap through which the wind came, and by crawling on his hands and knees he was able to squeeze through that opening.

He found himself in a passage that would have been too narrow for anyone much bigger than himself. Moving slowly, he felt his way between the twisting rock walls. Only the feel of the wind and the hope that it would lead to another way out, kept him moving onward. Then as suddenly as it had confined him, the passage opened up, and he stumbled into a rock chamber with a high ceiling, perhaps part of an old lava tube.

He let out an involuntary gasp. There it all was before him. The source of the wind was a small opening high up on a sheer wall. But a quick glance told Kai he wouldn't be able to reach it, or even if he did, it would be too small for him to get through.

Yet enough light filtered through that crack to illuminate the room with a dim, dusty clearness. Shafts of daylight played on objects piled against the walls. It was those objects that had caused Kai to gasp. The treasures of a burial cave! It was more than he could have imagined.

Against one wall were large wooden carved images. Tikis, many would call them, but Kai knew they were carvings of Hawaiian gods. Stacked around them were baskets woven of native materials, fragile and dusty with age.

The boy threw himself at the plunder as if he had been presented with a treasure chest. But with his first step he fell and sprawled to the ground, scraping his knees, and hurting his elbow. Rising slowly, he approached the materials with more caution and respect.

Perhaps he should leave these things to rest undisturbed, as they had remained for hundreds of years. He knew that was what his grandfather would say, yet he couldn't resist the temptation to see what was before him. So without a desire to take or to destroy, he stepped forward to look.

Brushing away the dust and cobwebs, he ran his fingers over the wooden form of one of the ancient god figures. The wood, although dried and cracked, was still whole. Nearly a foot tall, it was carved to resemble a human. Its large face had a fierce look, the mouth agape in a kind of snarl. Several other wooden figures lay to the side, and Kai picked them up gingerly, looking at each one.

Beside a wooden bowl, he noticed a small carved figure much like the bigger ones, but this one was only six inches high. He set it aside, having never seen anything that was so small and yet so carefully carved.

At the far end of the cave he bumped against a finely woven basket that hung from a wooden platform. He knew the basket might be the resting place for the bones of Hawaiian chiefs that must have been buried here. Not wishing to disturb the remains of the dead, he left the basket untouched.

Remembering how he had come to be in the cave, and wondering how much time had passed since Todd had left, Kai looked at his watch. But it had broken when he had fallen into the tree, and he couldn't tell the time. He hesitated, then turned to make his way out of the chamber. As much as he wanted to look at everything, he knew he had to be back on the ledge when Todd returned.

About to slip back into the narrow passage, Kai's glance fell again on the small carving of the ancient god. In an instant he had grabbed it and put it in his pocket, not knowing for sure why he wanted it, or what he would do with it, knowing only that he couldn't leave without taking something. Then he returned to the passage and retraced his steps to the cave's entrance.

As he climbed over the stones at the entrance, he saw that the sky was covered with clouds. A light rain had begun to fall, a prelude to what looked like a downpour. He moved back into the cave's sheltering mouth, worried that Todd might be delayed by the bad weather.

CHAPTER VI
Back On The Boat

It was after nine that morning when Mr. Parkson awoke on *Adventurer*. Had he known the trouble Kai and Todd were getting into, he would have sprung to life and tried to stop them. But he assumed they were on the boat, so, instead he rolled over and inspected the mess around him.

When the boat had nearly capsized the night before, clothes had fallen from the closets, drawers had slipped out of cabinets, books and charts had fallen out of their cases, and loose papers had scattered about the floor.

Mr. Parkson groaned and fell back onto the bed. After a short rest, he opened one eye to gaze at the ceiling where he wouldn't have to see the disorder. Then he raised himself on an arm and swung his legs off the bunk. There was lots of cleaning to do before the rest of the family arrived from town.

Expecting to hear the boys moving about, he paused, but heard only the gentle lapping of water beating against *Adventurer*'s hull. *The boys must still be asleep*, he thought, so he pounded the wall with the flat of his hand, "Wake up, you two."

Sliding his cabin door open, he walked into the main cabin where the disorder was even worse. It wasn't possible to avoid stepping on some of the broken plates, or the scattered pots and pans, cans of food, crackers, rice, and cookies. Opening the refrigerator door, a jumble of food fell out: broken eggs, spilled milk and orange juice, all mixed with the other food that had been inside the refrigerator.

He slammed the refrigerator shut and called sharply for the boys. When there was still no answer, he slid their door open, but the bunks were empty. "Where are they?" he said, also wondering how he was going to solve the immediate problem of preparing breakfast, and still concerned that the rest of the family, along with Kai's sister, would soon show up with Uncle Bob.

Heading for the deck, Mr. Parkson missed the note propped up for him on the table.

Everything on deck looked strangely deserted, and he began to feel the first touch of concern about Kai and Todd. Retreating to the cabin, he saw the note. It was in Todd's usual hurried scrawl and read:

Dear Dad,
> *We've gone horseback riding at a ranch*
> *down the road. Be back by noon.*
> > > *Todd*

"Horseback riding! Are you kidding?" Mr. Parkson bellowed in one of his loudest voices. Even though there was no one to hear him, it made him feel better to shout. "How could they just leave? They knew all this mess has to be cleaned up, and that the others are joining us this morning. Darn it all, we're supposed to sail to Kaua'i today."

In disgust and anger he threw the note on the table, then began to search the overturned jars for the one that held coffee beans. A good, strong cup of coffee would help him face the morning.

CHAPTER VII
Julie and Moana

By early afternoon a dark cloud had dumped a burst of rain on *Adventurer*, driving Mr. Parkson to the cabin below. After a few minutes the downpour lightened and he returned on deck where he gazed uncomfortably at his watch. It was now nearly two o'clock, and still no sign of the boys.

Not that he was really worried about their safety. After all, Kai had lived in Hawaii all his life and was probably familiar with the ranch they'd gone to. But it bothered him that they had left when there was work to do. That wasn't like either of them, and now they were way overdue.

"Oh, well," he grunted, realizing there wasn't much he could do and thankful that at least the boat was getting cleaned up with the help of the rest of the family who had arrived from town. "Julie!" he shouted into the main cabin. "Are you and Moana almost done in there? Your mother and Uncle Bob will be back shortly with the groceries."

"Yes, Dad," Todd's 11-year-old sister replied. Looking in a mirror, she checked to see if her ponytail was still neatly tied. Her freckled face stared back at her.

"Your hair looks good that way," said Moana, Kai's sister.

"Oh, thanks," Julie answered, trying to sound unconcerned, too embarrassed to admit that it was at least the tenth time that she had checked her new hair style. She pretended to run a rag over the mirror's surface, then allowed herself a smile. "Yes, I think so, too. Thanks for doing it this way."

Moana nodded and sank into one of the cushioned seats. They had been cleaning for nearly three hours, and she felt tired, hot, and dirty. The only break all morning had been when they had stopped to arrange Julie's hair, copying the style from a magazine they had found wedged behind the food locker.

For a moment Moana wondered where the boys were. She thought they must be doing something exciting. Kai seemed to always be getting himself and others into trouble with his exploring and adventures. She remembered the time they had all gone onto another boat that Kai had thought was being used to store stolen computer parts. Luckily, he had been right, and the boat owner was arrested. Otherwise, there could have been big trouble for them. She admired her brother, but sometimes he went too far. Now she felt worried that Mr. and Mrs. Parkson would get mad at him before the sailing trip to Kaua'i had even started.

The cheerful sound of Julie's voice brought her attention back. "We're finished cleaning," Julie said, as she looked around the cabin with pride. The mess that had greeted them that morning had been cleared away.

Three cardboard boxes were filled with broken plates, dishes, and ruined food. . . they would all have to be thrown out. The rest of the cabin shone. Things were put back where they belonged, furniture and cabinets had been cleaned, and the floor washed. It was the same in the three other cabins.

"Help me with this," Julie said, lifting the parrot's heavy metal cage to hang from a hook in the ceiling. From there, Kiddo, the parrot, could look out the port-hole. Stretching out one wing, then the other, Kiddo turned his head and began cleaning his green feathers.

The girls watched, fascinated by the bird. "I wish my parents would let me have a parrot," Moana said.

"They are fun," Julie agreed. She poked her finger in the cage, but the bird ignored her and continued to clean his feathers. "Lucky we had him with us at Uncle Bob's last night. From the way this cabin looked, his cage would have been tipped over if he had been on the boat." She tapped lightly on the cage to get Kiddo's attention.

"Hello, Julie," Kiddo replied.

Laughing at the bird, Moana stretched out on the couch. "I could use a shower," she said, and began rubbing at the film of sweat that covered her.

"How about a swim instead?" Julie suggested. She was always conscious about using too much fresh water from the boat's limited supply. "Then we could use the showers at the beach."

Moana readily agreed, and even before Mr. Parkson had finished saying they could go, the girls had tumbled into their cabin to change to swimsuits. Minutes later they were diving from the boat into the cool, green water of Kahana Bay.

"This is so great," Julie yelled. Refreshed by the water, she swam beside Moana toward the beach. A few minutes later she drew herself up on the sand, picked up a handful of it, and playfully threw it at her friend.

"I'll get you!" Moana shouted as the wet sand dribbled off her. She chased after Julie, who was running down the beach. Catching up to her, Moana threw a handful of sand. It landed on Julie's back, and laughing, the two girls fell into the shallow water.

"I know what we should do," Moana said, looking at the valley behind them. "Let's go back there. My grandfather's family used to live in that valley."

Julie shook her head negatively. She wasn't sure if she wanted to leave the beach and sight of the boat.

Pressing on with enthusiasm, Moana explained, "When I told my grandfather that we were coming here, he said there was a *heiau* nearby — that's a Hawaiian religious temple. He said our family used to worship there generations ago."

"I didn't think we'd have time to see it, so I didn't mention it before, but since your dad says we're not sailing to Kaua'i today, we could go to the *heiau*. It's just up the road. Come on, Julie," Moana urged, raising herself out of the water to see if she could spot the road that led to the temple.

"Are there any of your family that still live in the valley?" Julie asked.

"I don't think so, at least grandfather didn't say so. They all left years and years ago when there was a tidal wave. It smashed the houses and ruined our taro fields by making the ground too salty. That's when grandfather moved to where we live now. He was just a boy then, so it must have been at least fifty years ago."

"Do you think it would be OK to go up there?" Julie asked.

"Oh, sure. We won't disturb anything. We'll just walk along the road and see what's there."

The beeping of a car horn interrupted them. It was Julie's mother and Uncle Bob returning from their grocery shopping.

"OK," Julie agreed. "But let me ask Mom first." She ran over to where her mother and uncle were unloading groceries.

"Are the boys back?" Mrs. Parkson asked before Julie could say anything.

"No, Mom," Julie said. "And Moana and I want to walk up the road into the valley. Moana's grandfather used to live there."

"I guess so," Mrs. Parkson agreed as she set one bag of groceries to the ground then lifted another one from the car. "But don't be gone too long, and help us with these packages first."

When the rowboat was loaded, the girls gave it a push toward *Adventurer*. Then they turned and ran toward the valley.

From the rowboat, Mrs. Parkson gazed at the two girls in bare feet and bathing suits who were already receding behind the ironwood trees that lined the shore. For a moment she had second thoughts about letting them go. Raising her voice, she called loudly, "Be back in an hour."

CHAPTER VIII
Into The Valley

Moana and Julie ran under the tall ironwood trees that boarded the beach, paused before crossing the street, then started up a road that led into the valley. Smooth pavement soon turned into a rutted dirt road marked with pools of mud from the recent shower. Sunlight filtered through coconut trees that arched overhead. Birds chirped in the cool air, their sound joining that from a stream that flowed nearby. The mud squished between Julie's toes and she thought of throwing some at Moana, but resisted the temptation.

They passed a clearing where a small, wooden home stood. Rocking chairs stood on a wide *lanai* that faced the road, but no one sat in them now.

Just up the road they met a lady who smiled at them from her wrinkled face. Her heavy figure was wrapped in a loose, faded dress, the hem of which she held with one hand so it wouldn't drag in the mud. She also held a stick that she used to steady herself. In her other arm she cradled a crying baby.

Breathing heavily, the lady approached them, then broke into a surprisingly loud voice. "And what have we here? Two young visitors in our valley?"

Moana, remembering her parents' frequent advice not to talk to strangers, wasn't sure at first if she should ignore this person, or explain about her grandfather's family, or ask for directions to the *heiau*. Finally, she decided to ask for directions.

"Just ahead, just ahead, girls," the lady pointed. "Around the next bend, you'll find a path that goes off toward the stream. Follow that." She moved forward and eyed them more carefully, her look passing from Julie's white skin to Moana's dark brown color. "And what would you two want at a *heiau*?"

"My grandfather told us about it, and we just want to look at it," Moana said, edging away from the woman and motioning Julie to hurry along.

The woman watched them as they moved up the road. Before they were out of sight she called, "I'll be at the house down the road if you have any trouble."

Around the next bend, as the woman had described, the girls found a narrow path that seemed to lead toward the stream. A few steps along that route and the vegetation closed in, erasing all but a faint trace of the path. In the distance was the sound of the stream, so Moana pressed forward.

Behind her, Julie slipped and fell into a pool of mud, then bumped into a thick tree limb that grew across what remained of the trail. Because of Julie's grumbling, Moana was about to turn back, but decided to go on for just a few more steps.

Brushing away a pricker that felt like a bee sting, Julie thought of what they should have brought for this walk. She imagined supplies for an African safari: boots, long pants and shirts, sharp knives to clear the path, and mosquito repellent. Make that a large bottle of mosquito repellent, she decided as she slapped at another large blood sucker that had landed on her arm.

Then, abruptly, they stepped out of the underbrush and into a clearing. Here the greenery had been recently cut to a low level. Ahead the stream swept by, the clear water tumbling around and over rocks that had washed down the mountain. Above them arched large, shady tulip trees that dropped their reddish-orange blossoms onto the grass.

"This must be it," Moana said, spying the stone structure that lay ahead. Following her friend's glance, Julie saw gray and black rocks that had been carefully piled to form a square about five feet long on each side and three feet high.

"How do you know this is it?" Julie asked as she followed her friend around the structure. She didn't want to admit her disappointment, but it didn't look as she had pictured a Hawaiian religious temple would look. It looked more like... well, like a pile of rocks. Of course, she had only been in Hawaii a few months and never before had she even heard of a *heiau*, so she really had no idea of what one should look like.

She tried to imagine how she would describe it in her diary. Perhaps something like . . .

After a walk through the dark, mysterious jungle, where we feared that dangerous natives might attack us with their poison blow darts (she was thinking of the smiling

old lady), we came upon the lost temple. It
towered before us, bones of previous sacri-
fices scattered on top.

That would make a great movie, she thought to herself, but her vivid imagination was interrupted when
Moana began to explain the true facts. "This is what religious temples in Hawaii looked like. This would have
been a small one, a fishing shrine my grandfather said, I
think. The people would have left offerings of the fish
they caught and things like that on top." Moana spoke
confidently, remembering what she had learned in school
and also what she had heard from her grandfather.

After a few minutes of exploration, Moana allowed
herself to be coaxed back toward the path. "My ances-
tors lived around here," she said proudly, giving the
place one last look, and deciding that she would return
when she had more time to explore. She was glad she
had seen the *heiau.*

As they stepped from the path back onto the dirt
road, Julie agreed. "I'm glad I saw it, too, but the boys
should be back by now, and we promised Mom we
wouldn't be gone long." She didn't add that she had
begun to feel cold and was anxious to get out of the
damp woods.

Passing the house with the big *lanai,* Julie looked
up to see the woman they had met earlier. Now she
was sitting in one of the rockers. A baby cried from
inside the house and the lady's head snapped to attention. Julie lifted her hand in a friendly wave as she and
Moana went past.

The woman ignored the crying baby and sprang up, moving toward them. "Girls, girls! I've been waiting for you," she cried.

Puffing from the exertion, she reached the path and thrust her thick stick into the ground and leaned on it. "Did you find what you were looking for?" She smiled at them, brushing away the gray hair that had fallen across her face.

"Yes, thanks for the directions. My grandfather's family used to live in this valley. He told me about the *heiau*," Moana explained.

"Your grandfather? And who might that be?" The woman slapped at a mosquito that hovered near her face.

"Jeffrey Alau," Moana answered.

"Is that right? Well, now. . ." The woman said and stepped back, a surprised look on her face.

Recovering, the lady began, "I knew there was something about you. Something about you that looked familiar. . . the eyes I think. Oh, I knew your grandfather well, we grew up here together. Me on this land, and Jeffrey over there." She waved her hand toward the dense underbrush up the road. "No one has lived there for years, and I haven't seen Jeffrey in I don't know how long. He was back once for a party, but that must be at least ten or fifteen years ago."

"Yes, ma'am," Moana nodded. "He told me he hasn't been back in a long time. So that's where our family used to live?" She turned to look at the unkempt property.

"Yes, dear. The Alaus lived there for generations.

Your grandfather still owns that property, although the state would like us all to leave so they can make a park. Sixty years ago this valley was crowded with people, but a tidal wave chased most of them away years and years ago."

Her eyes glazed over with memories, then she continued, "Used to be that late afternoon like this would bring everybody home — the farmers, fishermen, and children from school. There'd be lots of happy noise, not like today when there's only a few families scattered through the whole valley. Now most of the people who live here are old like me."

Impatiently, Julie waited for the end of the conversation. Since they had stopped walking, the mosquitoes had discovered her again and were buzzing hungrily around. One landed on her swimsuit, and she swatted it. Coughing slightly to get Moana's attention, she said as politely as she could, "We'd better get going. We told Mom we wouldn't be long."

Moana nodded. "Good-bye. Thanks again for your help."

"Wait a minute," the woman said. "And is your grandfather still all right... in good health, I mean?"

"Yes."

"Good. Then you tell him that Matilda Kalahiki said 'Aloha,' and to get himself out here someday soon. And to bring his guitar. He used to be so good playing that guitar and singing."

"OK. But I won't see him for a few weeks. We're on our way to Kaua'i in my friend's sailboat. We're anchored in the bay now... that's why we came up here."

"All right, girls. But be sure and give your grandfather that message," Matilda said.

"Yes, ma'am. I'd like to come back, too."

"Aloha, girls. Aloha." The woman turned back to her home which could barely be seen in the late afternoon shadows that had begun to darken the valley.

"Come on, I'll race you," Julie challenged her friend. Neck and neck they charged along the muddy road, stopping only when they came onto the pavement. Julie scanned the bay, and saw *Adventurer*, swaying in the slight current.

CHAPTER IX
Rescued

At the base of Kualoa Mountain, Todd dodged the first rain drops. It had taken him longer than he had expected to reach the valley floor. Looking up at the steep cliffs above him, he tried to pick out the place where Kai was trapped, but it was too far away for him to be sure of the spot. "The horses, the horses," he repeated to himself as he looked for the place they had tied them.

Rain was now beginning to fall in a steady drizzle, and Todd pulled his shirt tightly around him as if it would keep him dry and warm. He realized that a heavy downpour would turn the mountain paths into mud, and make it difficult or impossible for him to climb back up the trail.

Seeing a group of trees that seemed familiar, he hurried toward them. The horses were there! They had edged themselves under those trees for protection from the rain. Now they nervously stomped the ground at Todd's approach, as if they sensed his worries.

The boy grabbed a coil of rope attached to the saddle of one of the horses. He wondered if it would be enough, but it would have to do. The only other rope was what secured the horses to the trees, and he couldn't take that.

Trying to feel confident, Todd readied himself for the trek back up the mountain, but he was consumed with doubt and worries. The mountain trail would be slippery from the rain. Should he go for help? How would he be able to pull Kai from that ledge? Resolutely, he started to retrace his steps. He didn't have all the answers, but maybe he could tie the rope to something so that Kai would be able to pull himself up.

Just as he reached the trail, he was startled by a gruff voice. "What you up to, brah?"

Surprised and scared, Todd turned to confront a man on horseback who was swathed in a rain slicker and wearing a wide brimmed cowboy hat. What could be seen of the Hawaiian man's face didn't look friendly.

"I've been watching to see if someone would return for these horses. Where you going, brah?" the man said.

"My . . . my friend . . ." Todd hesitated, then decided he would have to trust this stranger. "My friend fell on the mountain up there! I need the rope to rescue him."

A bolt of lightning flashed across the sky. The man steadied his horse, then turned back to Todd. "Is he hurt, your friend up there?"

Todd quickly explained how he had left Kai, apparently unhurt, but trapped on a ledge.

A minute later, the cowboy was pulling Todd up to sit behind him on his black stallion. "I'm a ranch hand here. I'll help you get your buddy." He introduced himself as Nathan.

With its two riders, the horse made its way ginger-ly up the mountain. Dripping wet and shivering, Todd held tightly to Nathan's waist. He was relieved that someone else was going to take charge of the rescue, and thankful that so far Nathan hadn't asked any uncomfortable questions about what they had been doing on the mountain.

When the trail got too steep for the horse, Nathan pulled the stallion to a halt and both riders got off. Shielding his eyes from the rain, Todd looked for the next pile of rocks he had left to mark the path he had taken down. Perhaps the rain had knocked them loose, or perhaps they'd missed that last pile. The horse had gone so quickly that it had been hard for him to spot the way.

"Come on, boy. We don't want to leave your buddy up there tonight. We only have a few hours left until dark," Nathan urged.

Looking in every direction, Todd finally saw the rocks he had left as markers. "That way," he said, trying to sound sure of himself.

It was another 15 minutes of hard climbing along muddy paths before they reached the ledge where the ground had given way beneath Kai's feet. Todd rushed forward to the edge of the cliff. "Kai! Kai! I'm, back!" he shouted. . . but there was no answer from below.

Beneath that ledge, Kai sat forlornly inside the mouth of the cave. Although the rain had just stopped, he wasn't able to shake his feelings of gloom. Perhaps something had happened to Todd, he had been gone so long. If his friend had fallen and was injured, how would anyone know to come to their rescue?

Shifting uncomfortably, he pulled out the small wooden figure that he had taken from the cave. The dust and dirt that had covered it for so many years easily rubbed away, but it wasn't so simple to decide what to do with it. He recalled stories his grandfather had told of bad luck happening to people who took such things for their own. But he had wanted to believe that misfortune wouldn't plague him since he respected the old ways.

Running his fingers lightly over the carving, he decided that for now he would tell only Todd of his discovery. No one else needed to know about the burial cave and its contents.

Lost in thought, he didn't hear his name being called from above. Then a louder voice woke him from his reverie.

"Brah! Hey, brah, are you down there?" Nathan called. Lying flat on the ledge above, he had inched part way out over the edge to get a view of what was below.

"Who's that?" Kai wondered, not recognizing the voice. He thrust the wooden figure into his pocket and climbed out of the cave. "I'm here!" he yelled more loudly.

"I've brought someone from the ranch to help you," Todd called in response.

Nathan was already busy tying one end of the rope to a stunted tree that grew nearby. Despite its scraggly appearance, the tree seemed to be strongly rooted. The man gave it a brutal tug to test its strength, and the tree held strong. At the rope's other end, he tied a loop, yanking it to check that it, too, would hold. Satisfied, he began to dangle the rope over the cliff, feeding it down foot by foot. "You'll have to climb out on that tree to grab hold of the rope. Then I'll pull you up," he shouted to Kai.

The cord tangled itself in the limbs of the tree, and carefully Kai began to edge toward it. As he reached the first low branches that bent out over the valley, he tried not to look down at the ground far below. For a moment, though, he did look, then felt so dizzy that he had to clench his eyes shut. He clung tightly to the trunk, afraid that somehow he would slip from the tree and fall downward.

"Come on, boy," Nathan called, sensing his hesitation. "You'll be all right. I've tied a loop in that rope for you to put your feet into... then just hold on and I'll pull you up. It'll be easy."

Kai opened his eyes. The sickening feeling remained. He wished he could return to the safety of the cool, dark cave, but he forced himself farther out into the tree. The rope was now only a foot away, and he could see the loop that the man had described.

"Are you sure you won't let me fall?" he asked. He avoided the temptation to look down.

"The rope is tied to a strong tree. You'll be fine," Nathan answered.

Forcing himself forward, Kai reached the thick cord and clutched it to himself. "I've got it!" he shouted.

"Good boy," Nathan answered. He was leaning dangerously over the cliff so he could see the teenager. "Now be real careful and put your foot inside that loop, then hold on tight," he said. "I'll pull you up, slow and sure."

Kai put his foot in the loop, but remained clinging to the tree, afraid to let go and swing out over the valley. He thought of his gym class when he had climbed the 25-foot rope to the gym's ceiling with never a thought of falling or letting go. He wanted to convince himself that this wasn't different. "Ready," he finally cried, loosening his grip on the tree.

Not daring to look down, he had the feeling he was falling through space as the rope swung him out over the valley and back toward the ledge where he crashed through the tree's branches.

The rope stabilized, and abruptly Kai was jerked upward as Nathan began to pull him in. With a few more strong pulls, he was looking over the ledge at Nathan and Todd.

"Hold on," Nathan grunted. Gathering in another handful of the rope, the man leaned down and pulled Kai onto the ledge.

"Thank God," Kai muttered, squirming away from the edge. With a tired smile, he looked up, "I made it! Thanks, you two!"

"You were lucky, brah," Nathan said and began to wind the rope around his arm. "If that tree hadn't been there, you would have fallen to your death. And I don't know how this skinny kid thought he was going to rescue you all alone." He looked suspiciously at Todd.

Kai nodded, breathing in great lung fulls of air, thankful that he didn't have to worry that the next breath might be the last he would ever take. He gave a silent prayer thanking God for his rescue. . . then once more thanked Todd and Nathan.

CHAPTER X
Back To The Boat

"What were you two doing here?" Nathan asked as he led the boys down the trail.

"I wanted to show my friend the view," Kai answered, not wanting to confess that they had been looking for caves, or to tell this man that he had actually found one. He thought it could lead to too many questions. He glanced at Todd, hoping he wouldn't be contradicted.

"The *view!* The view your friend almost had was of you falling to your death," Nathan said, then laughed, dismissing Kai's apparent foolishness. "OK, boys. Let's get you down the mountain to the horses, then back to your parents."

"But we're staying on a boat in Kahana Bay. We can catch the bus there ourselves." Kai tried to sound convincing since he didn't want the Parksons to find out what had happened.

"Oh, I'll take you. And one final bit of advice — stay off this mountain. It can be a dangerous place, as you've discovered."

After they had gotten their horses, ridden down

the mountain, and were approaching the stables, Kai reached into his saddle bag and pocketed the stone adze that he had found earlier that day. His pockets now bulged with the two treasures the mountain had revealed to him.

At the stables they piled into an old and tired-looking jeep that surprisingly sprang to life when Nathan turned the key. The jeep bumped down the rutted dirt road and joined the highway. The boys sat quietly on dusty leather seats, both worrying what Todd's parents were going to say.

Trailing a cloud of blue exhaust, the jeep clattered through the small town of Ka'a'awa and swung around a bend in the road to arrive at Kahana Bay where *Adventurer* swayed peacefully at anchor.

Even before they had come to a stop, Mr. Parkson was upon them. He strode angrily up to the jeep, "Where have you been? Your note said you'd be back by noon. It's almost six o'clock now."

The boys shuffled their feet in the dirt, their faces downturned, too embarrassed to look up. One glimpse of the adults told them how worried everyone had been.

"These boys got into some trouble on the mountain," Nathan broke the long silence. "One of them fell and had to be rescued."

"Whaaat? Their note said they were going horseback riding," Mr. Parkson stammered.

"That's right, but they left the horses and climbed pretty far up Kualoa."

Mrs. Parkson's face grew pale. "Are you both all right?" she asked.

"I'm fine. It's Kai who fell. We had to pull him up with a rope," Todd answered.

"I'm OK, too," Kai reassured them several times, while Nathan told of his rescue.

When everyone seemed satisfied that Kai was uninjured, Uncle Bob rowed the two hungry boys out to *Adventurer*, while Nathan returned to his jeep and clattered off.

Just as Nathan's jeep left the park, Julie and Moana raced out from under the trees. "Mom, Mom," Julie called.

"There you are," Mrs. Parkson smiled. She gathered her daughter in her arms, then made room for Moana. "We were getting worried about you two. Now everyone is back, safe and sound."

In the boat's galley, the boys busied themselves making something to eat. Todd piled fried Spam on top of lettuce, then started to make a second sandwich for Kai. "We haven't had anything to eat since this morning," he explained to Uncle Bob. "Chow time," he added, setting down the food laden plates.

As the boys wolfed down the first bites of their sandwiches, Uncle Bob stood up. "OK, you two. At least your appetites are all right. I've got to row back to shore and get the others."

When Uncle Bob had gone up the stairs, Kai stood and looked out the porthole. In a moment the rowboat glided past toward the beach. "Listen, I haven't told you everything," Kai began excitedly.

"What? You want more food?" Todd asked.

"No, it doesn't have anything to do with food. Up on the mountain, you know that ledge I landed on? You'll never believe what was behind it!"

"What?" Todd asked between mouthfuls of sandwich.

"A burial cave! When you left, I noticed there was a cave there so I decided to explore it in case there was another way out. Well, I found a burial cave, just like I said might be there. There was a roomful of statues, and all sorts of things." About to show Todd the wooden carving, he felt *Adventurer* swing sharply as the rowboat knocked into it. The voices of the others spilled over the deck as they climbed onboard.

"Where are those two?" Mrs. Parkson's voice carried through the boat.

"When I left them, they were in the galley eating half the groceries we bought today," Uncle Bob answered.

"Don't say anything about the cave! I'll tell you all about it later," Kai said just as Julie and Moana rushed in, anxious to hear what had happened to their brothers. Complaining of being tired, the boys managed to avoid another retelling of the accident.

"You're sure you're not hurt?" Mrs. Parkson asked Kai again. "I think we should take you to a doctor for a checkup."

Mr. Parkson looked irritated. "If the boy says he's all right, I don't see why we should go looking for a doctor. Heck, we'll never get to Kaua'i if we have to go back to Honolulu and see a doctor. How do you feel, Kai?" Mr. Parkson said.

"Fine, sir. Just a little tired and kind of sore from where I hit the tree," Kai answered.

"He says he's sore," insisted Mrs. Parkson, an alarmed tone to her voice. "He could have a broken rib, and at least we have to let his parents know that he had a bad fall, even if he is all right."

"Mom, Kai and I are going to lie down. We're **both** tired." Todd said. He emphasized the word 'both' since he felt no one was paying enough attention to him.

"All right, if Kai has bruised or broken ribs he should lie down," she agreed, still not paying any attention to Todd.

When the boys had retreated to their cabin and pulled its door closed, Kai took the carving from his pocket. "I found this in the cave," he announced.

At the sight of the sculpture, Todd, who had just stretched out in the lower bunk, jumped up. "Let me see it," he said. He ran his hands over the smoothly polished wood and around the sculpture's mouth, which to his eyes had a snarling, mean look.

"What are you going to do with it? It makes me feel *spooky*," he said, handing it back as Kai told about the other things he had seen in the cave.

"I don't know what I'll do with it," Kai answered. "My grandfather would say never go into a burial cave, and absolutely never take anything from one. But I just couldn't resist this. I hope we won't have bad luck because of it." He leaned against the cabin wall, holding the carving up to the late afternoon light that streamed in through the porthole.

"What do you mean *bad luck*?"

"Oh, that's what people say about things like this. If you take Hawaiian things from where they belong, you're supposed to have bad luck, like having accidents and getting sick, stuff like that. But I'm not planning to harm it." He looked closely at the carving and seemed to be speaking as much to it as to Todd.

"Seems to me, we already had our bad luck when you fell off that cliff," Todd objected.

Dismissing the other's concern, Kai crawled onto the top bunk. "Hey, brah, I'd call it good luck to find this carving and the adze, too." He rolled over to go to sleep, but the stone adze in his pocket pinched against him. He took the adze out, dropping it onto Todd's desk where it landed with a heavy thud. Moments later, both boys were asleep.

CHAPTER XI
A Sudden Storm

In the main cabin the Parksons were discussing the day's events. "With the groceries you both bought, we can pull up anchor and start to Kaua'i," Mr. Parkson said.

"You don't mean now, do you?" his wife asked.

"No, but tomorrow as long as the weather looks good. There's no reason to stay here longer," Mr. Parkson said.

Mrs. Parkson clasped her hands in front of her. She had the look of someone who had made up her mind and would put up with no nonsense. "I want to take Kai to a doctor before we start the trip. Now I've said it, and I mean it. He could have some internal injuries. We don't want to get out on the ocean and then realize that he's hurt."

After a long pause, Mr. Parkson agreed. "You're probably right. In any case, I had planned to go ashore tonight and call his parents."

He turned to his brother who had lived in the islands for many years. "Bob, are there any doctors around here? Maybe we could get this all taken care of tonight."

"There's a hospital about ten miles up the road. They'd have an emergency room and could check Kai," Uncle Bob answered.

"Fine! Then, if everything's all right, we can still sail tomorrow," Mr. Parkson agreed.

"Arooha, arooha, squawk, squawk," the parrot leaped from one bar to another in his cage. "Arooha, arooha."

Everyone stopped to listen to Kiddo's mastery of the Hawaiian greeting. Julie stuck her finger through the bars of the cage and gently touched the bird's feathers. "Aloha, Kiddo, aloha," she corrected him.

"Hi, Julie. Hi, Julie," Kiddo responded.

"Mom," Julie said, "Do Moana and I have to go to the hospital? Can't we play on the beach? We'll be good, honest."

"Oh, Julie, it's dark now, and I don't want to leave you two alone on the beach at night," her mother said.

Before Julie could say anything more, her uncle broke in. "I'll stay with the girls," he offered. "You two take the car. The hospital is along the main road so you won't have any trouble finding it. I'd rather sit on the beach. I don't get out this way very often."

"Yes! Maybe we can even have a bonfire," Julie shouted, embracing her uncle.

Uncle Bob nodded in a surprised way.

"OK," Mr. Parkson agreed. "But we better get started. I'm afraid those boys are going to be too tired tomorrow to be much help in sailing." He walked over to their door and knocked lightly. There was no response, so he knocked again.

Kai was sleeping restlessly, dreaming he was in a room full of statues of ancient gods. The statues seemed to be leaning over him in a threatening way. To show his respect, he followed the ancient custom of throwing himself face down on the ground. He could hear someone beating on what sounded like a drum and shouting, "Get up. Get up." Then he woke and realized that Mr. Parkson was knocking on the door and calling for him and Todd to get up.

Sliding off his bunk, Kai felt his pocket. Yes, the carved figure was still there, but both he and Todd forgot the adze that lay on the desk. Moments later, they were in the car heading away from the bay for the hospital, leaving their sisters and Uncle Bob on the beach.

The girls busied themselves with collecting dead branches from under nearby trees, while Uncle Bob cleared a place for the fire. The first stars had just become visible against a sky which had turned from dark blue to black when the flames from the fire shot up. Julie and Moana edged into its yellow light.

"This sure is nice," Julie said, pulling her sweater tight against the steady wind that blew in from the ocean. When the girls' eyes had become accustomed to the darkness, they finished collecting firewood, then began to play among the trees.

Uncle Bob stepped away from the crackling flames to look at the stars. He was surprised to see that the sky had become covered with low clouds. Straining his eyes, he looked from one end of the bay to the other, but couldn't make out *Adventurer*. A misty cloud hung over the spot where the boat was anchored.

An increasing wind brought with it the first drops of rain, and the once quiet surf began to pound against the beach with a boom that echoed over the valley. The girls retreated to the fire, huddling there, wishing for more shelter.

"Just our luck. . . a storm is blowing in," Uncle Bob said as he tried to keep the fire going despite the rain. He looked toward the bay, hoping that the sky would begin to clear, but instead the storm seemed to intensify. A stinging rain, blown by a strong wind, beat against them.

Trying to shelter the fire, Uncle Bob stood up and caught sight of the rowboat as it was being pounded by the rising waves. "Come on, girls, quick! The rowboat is about to float off!" he shouted.

He led them into the surf which had come up to the highest levels of the beach and was beginning to wash among the trees. By the time they had wrestled the light boat to higher ground, they all were wet to the skin, and when they returned to the fire, it had gone out.

The wind blew at them with a moaning sound, the air full of rain and small branches that had broken off trees. For a moment Uncle Bob wondered if they should run out to the road and try to flag down a passing car that could take them to shelter, but then he realized that no cars had gone by since the storm had surprised them. Anyway, he felt sure that this squall would pass as quickly as it had appeared, as so many storms in Hawaii do. Even so, he knew they shouldn't stand out in the open like they were, so he grabbed the girls and led them to the shelter of some large trees.

Crouching against the trunk of an ironwood tree,

Julie licked her lips. She could taste the salt from the ocean spray. Water trickled off the tree trunk and down her clothes. It was uncomfortable, but when she leaned away from the trunk, the full force of the wind and rain hit her, and that was worse.

Then she remembered their boat. "*Adventurer!*" she shouted, as she stood and tried to see into the bay. "I hope it's OK. Oh, it will be a mess all over again." She was thinking of the portholes they had left open, and the wind and rain that would have entered the cabins.

Moana and Uncle Bob pressed against her, also trying to see out to the boat, but the lashing rain made it impossible to see even as far as the rowboat. "Poor Kiddo. It must be awful out there," Moana said.

With a loud boom, a nearby tree cracked and fell. Branches of all sizes whistled past them. Uncle Bob forced the girls down, pushing them even closer to the tree trunk for their protection. He, too, thought of *Adventurer*, and hoped that it was properly anchored. *Where were the Parksons? Shouldn't they, too, have felt the storm and returned?*

In the next moments, sea water began to pour into the gully where they were crouched. They made a dash to higher ground, again finding shelter behind large trees. All three chattered with cold. Their clothes were soaking wet, and they were beginning to worry for their own safety.

A sudden gust of wind sent something large flying past. In the flickering light of a street lamp, Uncle Bob thought it looked like the rowboat. Whatever it was, it careened onto the highway, breaking apart. The wind picked up the plastic pieces and blew them off into the valley.

Bending out from behind the tree, Uncle Bob peered toward the bay. The storm was passing now. That last gust seemed to have been its final blow. He looked for *Adventurer*, but his glasses were so wet that he could barely see anything other than a large white object close to shore. "Julie, take a look out there," he said.

Obligingly, his niece peered out from the tree. She, too, could tell that the worst of the storm was over. The sky was clearing, and she could see out to the bay and beyond to where the ocean broke against the reef. But where was *Adventurer*? Her stomach lurched with nervousness and fright, as if she had returned home to find her house missing from its yard. Why wasn't the boat where they had anchored it?

Scanning the bay, she saw an old white boat, over-turned on the beach about fifty yards away. She didn't remember seeing that before, but her eyes passed over it, knowing it couldn't be the proud form of their sailing yacht. Yet, the rest of the bay was empty, and her glance returned to that overturned hull.

"There's a boat over there, but I don't think it's ours," she said with a sickening feeling, wishing that she believed her own words. With an uncomfortable start she recognized the thin, black, painted line around *Adventurer*'s hull.

"Oh, no!" she thought, *"It IS Adventurer!"*

Their boat lay on its side in shallow water, its mast broken, the water lapping nearly into the cabin.

CHAPTER XII

Damage

The rain and wind had passed as suddenly as they had appeared at Kahana Bay. From the shelter of the trees, the three survivors stared out at a changed scene.

The park was littered with broken tree limbs and the trunks of several large ironwood trees that had fallen over. The girls and Uncle Bob maneuvered around picnic tables that lay overturned and rubbish cans that had rolled on their sides, their wet contents covering the grounds. Behind them, a car skidded around pieces of the smashed rowboat, then passed on.

Julie kept hoping that it was a trick of her mind that made the marooned boat look like *Adventurer.* She couldn't accept the idea that she was the victim of a disaster like the ones she had seen on the TV news when people lose their homes in a hurricane or tornado.

When she looked around, she half expected that a TV news camera would be waiting to poke its nosy way onto their ruined boat. Surely the sight of this wreck would attract curious spectators, and she felt embarrassed by that.

Always so proud of *Adventurer*, now she dreaded the thought that people would want to look at it because it was wrecked. It looked so awful. Part of her wanted to run and hide, but instead she and the others waded out toward the overturned boat.

Adventurer's deck was tipped in their direction, and in the dark everything looked almost normal, except for it being on its side. Life preservers were still attached to the cabin, the brass around the portholes glistened in the starlight, and even Todd's jacket was still tied where he had left it on the safety line that ran around the deck. Now a gentle breeze lifted the jacket, which flapped against itself like a flag.

As the wind pushed the last clouds away from the moon, it was Moana who saw the real damage. "Oh, my gosh, the mast fell onto the cabin!" she gasped.

Going closer, the three saw that Moana was right. The boom of the mast had crashed into the cabin. Julie tried to imagine what it must be like inside the boat, but couldn't. She wasn't even sure which part had been damaged. Was it her cabin, Todd's, or the main cabin?

"Everything must be soaked inside," Moana groaned as they looked over the stern. The cabin door, which was knocked partly off its hinges, swung back and forth with the waves that washed onto the boat.

Trying to lighten everyone's feelings, Uncle Bob said he thought the boat could be repaired since there didn't seem to be any real damage to the hull. Julie nodded, trying to feel hopeful, then she remembered the parrot.

"Kiddo!" she shouted, and before anyone could stop her, she had pulled herself onto the boat and was wading through sloshing water toward the cabin. Her uncle yelled at her to come back.

"Kiddo's inside!" she replied, thinking only of rescuing their green parrot.

Behind her, Uncle Bob pulled himself onto the boat. Struggling to his feet, he tried to keep his balance on the sloping deck as Julie yanked the cabin door aside.

"Kiddo, Kiddo," she cried softly. The door, loosened by the storm, broke off in her hands and floated away in a pool of water. Poking her head inside the cabin's dark interior, Julie could hardly see a thing. Only a few impressions registered. . . the sound of water gurgling around the floor, and the cabin roof smashed open to the night sky. About to step down the stairs, she felt her arm grabbed.

"You're not going into that mess! It's too dangerous in there. We'll wait on shore until your father returns." Her uncle forced her away from the door and then back over the boat's side.

Julie angrily protested and twisted her arm free. If Kiddo needed her help, it wouldn't be right to delay. But her uncle and Moana led her away from the boat, then put their arms around her to comfort her. She began to cry, realizing that the bird hadn't answered her calls with his usual chatter. There had only been silence.

CHAPTER XIII
At The Bay

As the cooling night air blew in through the car window, Mrs. Parkson leaned back with satisfaction. Now she could relax. The doctor had given Kai a quick examination and found him to be fine. Tomorrow they could be on their way to Kaua'i.

For twenty minutes, the car followed the winding country road that led from the hospital to Kahana Bay. There was little traffic, and lulled by a warm breeze, the boys soon fell asleep.

It was Mr. Parkson who first suspected that something might be wrong. Rounding a final curve, the car's headlights shot out over the bay. Mr. Parkson looked out, expecting to see his boat, but *Adventurer* wasn't there.

Surprised, he braked the car to a crawl and leaned out the window, searching the water for the familiar shape of the boat. Could this be a different bay? Could Uncle Bob have moved the boat for some reason?

Feeling the first touch of concern, he jammed down on the gas pedal. The car sped toward the park, jolting the boys awake. Mrs. Parkson looked up. "What's wrong, honey?" she asked.

Too worried to answer, Mr. Parkson swerved to avoid hitting some smashed plastic that he never would have recognized as his own rowboat. The car's headlights picked out shattered trees, overturned garbage cans, and smashed picnic tables. It was a scene of disaster. *"What the heck...What's happened here?"* he said to himself.

As he struggled to loosen his seat belt, Julie, her wet clothes hanging heavily on her, came running into the beam of the headlights. "We've got to get to the boat and rescue Kiddo! Hurry, Daddy! Bring a flashlight!" she yelled.

Then a mud-spattered Uncle Bob, followed by a dripping and chattering Moana, appeared out of the darkness. Breathlessly, Uncle Bob told about the storm.

"Storm, what storm?" Mrs. Parkson got shakily out of the car.

Always quick to react, Mr. Parkson grabbed the flashlight from under the car seat and followed his daughter through the mud and debris to the beach. There he saw *Adventurer* laying on its side in shallow water.

Julie led the way into the water, her father slogging after her, playing the beam of the flashlight over the boat as he checked for damage. "Hurry, Daddy," Julie cried, lifting herself onto *Adventurer*.

"Wait there," Mr. Parkson ordered and pulled himself onto the deck beside her. He made his way toward the doorway and dropped into the main cabin.

Landing with a thud against the port side, he twisted his ankle on the overturned stove. A foot of water swirled through the dark interior, and there was the stench of oil and gas that must have leaked from the auxiliary engine and generator tanks. An eerie silence pervaded the cabin. The only sound was the water as it swirled around their personal belongings.

Pushing aside the debris that floated past, Mr. Parkson ducked beneath the broken roof and aimed his flashlight along the walls and floor looking for Kiddo's cage. It wasn't only Julie who was concerned about Kiddo. He, himself, had bought the bird in San Diego, and they were all attached to their feathered pet.

Eventually he found the smashed ceiling beam from which Kiddo's cage had been suspended, but the cage had broken loose. Then, underneath part of the mast, he saw the cage... crushed and half submerged in water. And still inside was Kiddo's lifeless body.

Tears clouded Mr. Parkson's eyes as he pulled the cage free. He reached in and took the dead parrot, wrapping it in a towel that he found on a high shelf. As he turned back toward the door, he saw Julie. She had seen everything, and stood weeping.

CHAPTER XIV
Into The Valley

The next morning dawned clear and bright. They were all surprised to see the sun come up as usual to shine on a calm, blue sea that sparkled under the sunlight. None of those who gazed out at *Adventurer* would have expected such a day. Somehow, cloudy, rainy, miserable weather would have better expressed their feelings.

It had been a difficult night. Except for short breaks to rest, they had all worked continuously to bring ashore what could be salvaged from *Adventurer* before it was ruined by the water.

Now the car was surrounded with the things that they had sorted and piled. In one pile were the things they could save — like wet clothing, kitchen utensils, and a few unbroken dishes. Other things that would have to be thrown out lay in a large pile that kept getting bigger.

As the sun rose above the clouds low on the horizon, the boys slipped off with a shovel and headed up the road into the valley.

A little later, the others put aside their work and followed Julie across the highway and onto the dirt road that would take them to Moana's grandfather's property. In her arms, Julie cradled Kiddo's body wrapped in a towel.

From the home of Matilda, the Hawaiian lady, came the pleasant aroma of eggs and bacon cooking. But there was no one in the yard, and the sad party didn't pause. Around the bend the boys waited dutifully by the hole they had dug.

The family said their good-byes quickly. Julie didn't cry anymore. She had done much of that through the night and now she felt somehow satisfied that Kiddo would be resting in such beautiful and peaceful surroundings.

Her mother put her arms around her as they walked back toward the boat. "We'll always have the memories of the dead. We'll never forget Kiddo, so in a way he's still with us," she said. Julie nodded, trying to accept that comfort.

When they came around the turn in the road, Matilda was standing at the edge of her yard. "Aloha," she seemed to breathe the greeting to them. "Aloha. I wondered where you all were going so early in the morning. Come in and eat. Have some breakfast." She put her arm around Moana's waist. "You know, we're related. Your grandfather and I are distant cousins, so that makes us some sort of relation."

Moana introduced Matilda to the others, and everyone allowed themselves to be ushered toward the house.

"Just me home this morning. I'm not taking care of my neighbor's baby today, but my son will be back

in a while. I told him about meeting Moana, but I was afraid I might not see her again." She pulled Moana closer to her.

Embarrassed to be the center of attention, Moana grabbed at Kai, who followed behind. "This is my brother. So if I'm related to you, he is, too," she said.

"Well, well. Finding two relatives in a day, that's real luck! We need to celebrate. And were you showing your grandfather's property to your brother?" Matilda asked.

"I hope you don't mind," Moana whispered. "We needed a place to bury Julie's parrot, so I suggested grandfather's land."

"Ahhh," Matilda nodded. "I thought you all looked sad when you went past earlier. You were so quiet on such a pretty morning. Of course it's all right to use that property, it's yours. And it's a wonderful place for a pet to be." She reached out and pulled Julie to her to comfort her.

Julie buried her face in the woman's bosom and allowed the tears to flow. In a moment she felt better and looked up into brown eyes that gazed with understanding into her own.

"You'll just have to show me where that grave is so I can take care of it," Matilda suggested.

"All right," Julie agreed.

"How'd you people get through the storm? There doesn't seem to be any damage here," Mr. Parkson asked, glancing around Matilda's neat yard.

"What storm?" Matilda said.

"Last night's. The one that blew our boat onto the beach."

Matilda looked puzzled. "We didn't have any storm. Maybe a little rain, but no big storm."

"What? Our boat is overturned in the bay, the park is a mess, and you say there was no storm here?" Mr. Parkson said.

"That's right. I'm sorry if your boat was damaged, but you can see there was no big storm here," Matilda repeated. She gestured to her yard where only a few piles of raked leaves marred the neatness. "That happens though. Bad weather sometimes hits just a small part of the island."

"You know, now that I think of it, when we walked up the road this morning, I didn't notice any damage outside the park," Uncle Bob observed.

"And on the way back from the hospital last night, there wasn't any damage either. Not a hint of rain or wind until we got to the park," Mr. Parkson recalled.

Matilda shrugged her shoulders. "Stranger things have happened in these islands and in this valley. Now come in and let me make you a good Hawaiian breakfast. Sounds like you need it."

The seven of them sat around the large kitchen table as Matilda busied herself at an old stove. "No, you just sit there and rest. I can see you're tired," she said when Mrs. Parkson offered to help. "Besides, I know where everything is, and for us Hawaiians it's a pleasure to cook for lots of people. But I will ask my new family to help just a little." She beckoned to Moana and Kai, who loaded the table with pitchers of milk and orange juice, followed by a steady stream of platters of rice, eggs, potatoes, Spam, fish, and poi.

When everyone had eaten their fill, Matilda sat and poured them all steaming cups of coffee. Eagerly counting the cups, Julie waited until the adults had gotten theirs, then grabbed one for herself and began to drink before anyone could forbid it. Her mother gave her a startled look, but didn't say anything.

Matilda looked approvingly at the empty plates. Like any good cook, she was pleased when people ate a lot.

"From the way you describe it, there must be one mess down at the bay," she said. "Sorry I can't help you clean up, but my son will be here soon. He'll help you. He's a big man, and very strong."

About to refuse, Mr. Parkson decided that an extra pair of hands might come in handy. Then, remembering that someone from the insurance company could appear at any time to look at the boat's damage, he thanked Matilda, and explained why he had to leave. Uncle Bob and Mrs. Parkson joined him at the door.

"You kids stay here and help Matilda clean up," Mrs. Parkson said. With their good-byes and thank-yous exchanged, the adults passed through the yard and turned down the road toward the beach.

CHAPTER XV
Stories Of Long Ago

As soon as Matilda had seen the adults leave her yard, she turned anxiously to the girls. "You two didn't take anything from that *heiau*, the religious temple you visited yesterday, did you? I didn't want to worry your parents, so I didn't say anything, but I can't remember when a storm has hit the bay and not up here. That seems very peculiar to me. And so I sat thinking, how could that happen? Why should bad luck fall on these people? And just yesterday you two girls went up to that *heiau*. Did you take anything, children? Even a little rock?"

"Oh, no, Ma'am. I know better than to do something like that," Moana replied. Both she and Moana looked at Julie, who shook her head negatively.

"Good," Matilda said. "I didn't think you looked like the kind who would, but today you never know. There are so many foolish people in the world. And all the stories about bad luck and accidents that happen to people who take things from the old places. *Auwe*," she whistled softly under her breath. "We wouldn't want that to happen to you."

Had Matilda looked at the boys just then, she would have noticed the anxious looks on their faces. Todd's complexion had turned pale with concern, while Kai's forehead was etched with lines of concentration and worry. Both were thinking of the cave and the wooden carving that Kai had taken from it, as well as the adze that he had found. Instinctively, Kai reached into his pocket and ran his fingers over the carving that he was carrying with him.

"I. . . I. . . I," Todd stumbled over the words as he might trip over his own feet if he were fleeing a house full of ghosts. He felt he should tell Matilda about the things he and Kai had found on the mountain. "I guess the girls didn't find anything, but . . ."

Suspecting that Todd was about to tell what they had found, Kai let go with a solid kick under the table. It did the job. Todd shut his mouth after a muffled, "Ouch."

The boys were spared an embarrassing explanation of their behavior when the sound of heavy feet pounded up the front steps. A gruff voice called, "I'm home, Mom," followed by the sound of boots being pulled off, and the padding of bare feet toward the kitchen.

"Nathan, these are some children I've met. You'll never believe what happened to them," Matilda said.

"Nathan!" Todd and Kai exclaimed at once as they turned to see the big Hawaiian man who had rescued them the previous day.

"Ha, ha, ha!" he laughed. "Yes, I know what these boys have been up to. These are the same two I told you I had to rescue on the side of the mountain."

"Glory be," Matilda gasped. "What a family! You children certainly lead an action-packed life. Just like a TV show, falling down a mountain one day, and your boat rolling over the next."

"What's this about the boat?" Nathan pulled a chair up to the table and turned a questioning look toward the boys. But they were too stunned at seeing him to answer, so Julie briefly explained what the storm had done to *Adventurer*.

Nathan listened while loading a plate with eggs and rice. "That's strange. There wasn't any storm up here," he said.

"That's just what we were talking about," Matilda answered. "Anyway, I told their parents that you'd help them clean up."

"Sure, Mom," Nathan said.

"And these two are your relatives. I told you about the girl last night, now I find out she has this brother." Matilda indicated Kai and Moana.

"So it was my own relative I saved on that mountain," Nathan said.

Kai nodded glumly. He couldn't get his mind off what Matilda had said about bad luck happening to people who take things from the old places. Could the carving he had taken have something to do with the storm? As the girls talked with Nathan and Matilda, he sat wondering what he should do.

When Nathan had finished eating, and the four young people had helped to clean the dishes, they all packed themselves into the jeep for the short ride to the beach. Julie promptly began bombarding Nathan with the same questions that were occurring to Kai, questions about bad luck happening to people who took things from a temple.

"That's what people believe," Nathan agreed.

"Matilda thought we might have taken something from the *heiau*, and that could have caused the storm," Julie said. "She said it wasn't normal for a storm to hit just in the bay and not up at your house."

"That's true, too. Did you take anything?" Nathan asked sharply.

"No, of course not," the girls answered together.

"But could something like that really happen?" Julie asked. She had lived almost all her life in San Diego, so these beliefs were new to her. It didn't seem possible to her that bad things would happen because someone took an old rock.

"So you're curious about our beliefs?" Nathan said, glancing at her with interest as the jeep came to a stop in the park. "It's the ancient gods and their power we're talking about," he explained. "They cause the bad luck. Remember that those gods were worshipped here for hundreds of years, and there are still people who believe in them. I think all Hawaiians believe in some of the old religion, even though most of us go to church at least once in a while."

"Sure, strange things still happen here in Hawaii," he continued. "Things like people having bad luck after they take something they shouldn't, or after they go into some forbidden, *kapu*, place. Everyone who has lived here long enough knows stories like that. Even *haole* people believe them."

"Do you believe those things?" Julie asked, mystified.

"Of course. What do you think I've been telling you? And there's also the stories about, *ka huaka'i po*, nightmarchers. Those are the spirits of the old Hawaiians who reappear on certain nights."

"Nightmarchers! You mean there really are such things?" Todd said. He was remembering that Kai had thought the torches they had seen on the side of Kualoa were carried by nightmarchers. "Do you believe in nightmarchers?" he asked again.

"Sure, I believe in them. Everybody does," the man laughed.

Sensing Todd's excitement, and afraid again that he would tell about the cave and what he had taken from it, Kai gave his friend a push that sent him sprawling out of the parked jeep.

Sputtering with surprise, Todd got up, but before he could say anything, Kai had jumped out and was helping to dust him off.

"Sorry, brah. One bee was about to sting me, that's why I pushed into you," Kai said. He bent closer and whispered, "Come on, we've got to get into the boat and get the adze."

Kai looked out at *Adventurer*. The receding tide had left it almost dry on a sandbank. Did the damage to the boat have something to do with the things they had taken? He couldn't take any chances, they would have to find a way to put the adze and the carving back on the mountain.

"Come on," he urged again, heading for the beach.

CHAPTER XVI
The Missing Adze

Urged on by Kai, Todd strode along the beach past his father and the man he was talking to. "We're going onto *Adventurer*," Todd called, wading into the shallow water.

"Wait a minute," Mr. Parkson yelled back. "This man is from the insurance company, and he'll want to check the damage on the boat before you get in there again."

The water lapping around their feet, the boys stopped. "What about our things in the cabin?" Todd asked.

His father turned to the insurance man before answering. That man's voice came clearly over the water, "I can tell it's a water spout that hit you. They're just like tornadoes, except they form over water. And like tornadoes they can do damage to small areas like was done here." He shuffled through some papers in his briefcase, looked out at the water between him and the boat, then down at his expensive leather shoes and clean long pants. "I don't really need to see inside the boat. Why don't you just tell me what's damaged?" he decided.

"Fine," Mr. Parkson agreed. Both men turned and

started toward the things piled beside Uncle Bob's car.

"Dad, can we go, or what? The tide is real low so we can get into the cabins now," Todd called to the retreating figures.

Mr. Parkson waved back at them, "Sure. Go ahead, but be careful. And bring out as much as you can. All that wet clothing is going to have to be cleaned."

A moment later, Kai was pulling himself onto *Adventurer*'s sloping deck, then over to the stairs that tilted crazily down toward the cabins.

He knew his decision was right. The adze and the carving would have to be returned to the mountain, and the sooner the better. He wasn't sure if taking those things had been the cause of the storm, but he didn't want to chance any more bad luck.

The boys dropped into the main cabin. Most of the water had already been drained out by a hand pump, but a musty odor was still unpleasantly noticeable. They shuffled through the sand and mud that lay underfoot and stepped over the refrigerator that had come loose and lay on its side. Above them hung the built-in table and benches that were permanently attached to the starboard wall. Kai couldn't help crouching, as if that built-in furniture might somehow come loose from the overturned boat and topple on him.

Making their way up the narrow hallway, they could see water still swirling around Mr. and Mrs. Parkson's things in the forward stateroom. Todd yanked on the door of his own cabin, and it slid open with a jerk that threw him forward. Water covered the floor so he retreated to get the pump. Peeking in, Kai saw that, other than the water, things didn't look too bad. The mattresses and bedding had come loose, but nothing had fallen out of the closet and drawers.

Todd returned, dropped the pump hose to the floor, and began to move the handle up and down. The water swirled and gurgled as it was sucked out.

"Wait a minute! Wait a minute!" Kai pushed his friend from the pump. "I want to find that adze before it's sucked through the hose." He dropped into the cabin, threw the hose out the door, and ran his hand under several inches of sand that covered the floor. "Come on, help me. We left the adze on the desk. . . it has to be here someplace," he said.

In the small room the boys checked and rechecked the same places. But after fifteen minutes of searching, Kai had to admit that the adze wasn't there and there was no place else to look. "Oh, no — it's gone," he said.

"Could the storm and the missing adze have any-thing to do with what Nathan was talking about — those spirits, nightmarchers, and stuff? Like those spirits want those things you took?" Todd asked.

Kai tried to look like he didn't believe it, although he had been thinking the same thing for the last hour. "Nah, but maybe we shouldn't have taken them," he answered, beginning to worry that he might be blamed for the boat's damage.

"Taken what?" a familiar, gruff voice asked from the door.

The boys looked up to see Nathan peering in at them. Then Julie and Moana went past and began pulling on the door to their cabin. "Help us with this,

Nathan. It's stuck," Julie said.

Without waiting for the boys to answer his question, Nathan yanked on the girls' door. It opened, releasing a pool of water that splattered them all.

Edging away from the door and into a corner where no one except Todd could see him, Kai pulled the carving from his pocket. "The adze is gone. Now we'll have to get rid of this," he said. He gazed at the wooden figure and ran his fingers over its sharp angles. "I suppose I never should have taken it, but I didn't think any harm would come because of it."

Todd fanned himself. The cabin was hot and stuffy, and he didn't know if he liked being involved in things he didn't understand. He gave the room another search, then admitted that somehow the adze had disappeared. "OK, we'll return the carving, but there's a problem. Mom and Dad will never let us go back to that ranch after what happened to you the last time."

For a moment Kai was silent. He, himself, didn't really want to go near the cave again. Besides, with only Todd to help, he wouldn't be able to get back from the cave to the ledge above. They couldn't do it alone.

"We could take the carving up to that stone temple, the *heiau*, the girls saw yesterday. Let's leave it there," Kai suggested. "It's a sacred, religious place, and it would be almost like returning it to the cave. At least we wouldn't have it anymore."

"I guess so. If you're sure that would be the right thing to do," Todd agreed.

Before Kai could answer, a scraping noise silenced them both. With Nathan's help, the girls were pulling a chest full of their belongings along the corridor. When they had passed, Kai said, "Yeah, that's what we'll do. It will be all right at the *heiau*, I'm sure. So if we're going up there, we'd better get started."

"Now?" Todd asked.

"The sooner the better," Kai said, and led the way to the deck. Their thoughts on the missing adze and the carving, the boys waded toward shore where the adults were going through the girls' chest of wet clothing.

"Where are your things, boys?" Mr. Parkson called.

"Huh, Dad?" Todd said, puzzled.

"Your things. You were supposed to bring everything out from the boat."

"Oh, we forgot," Todd said.

"Listen, son, I have a good mind to make you march right back to that boat and finish your work," Mr. Parkson said, a frustrated tone to his voice.

"Yes, sir," Todd replied, his eyes downcast. Turning back toward *Adventurer*, he motioned Kai to join him.

"Oh, never mind. Nathan has invited you kids to have lunch at his house, and I don't want to hold him up. Uncle Bob and I will get the rest of the things," Mr. Parkson said.

Todd nodded his agreement and headed for Nathan's jeep. Kai hesitated, then realized that going to Nathan's would be the perfect opportunity to go to the *heiau* and hide the carving. He ran to join the others.

With Nathan driving and the four young people crowded into the seats, the jeep bounced up the valley road, and then into Nathan's yard. It was clear Matilda wasn't home. The doors and windows of the house were all shut.

"Mom must have gone out for a while. No problem, I'll make lunch. It'll just take a few minutes, " Nathan said.

"We'll help," Julie volunteered for herself and Moana. She was curious to see how this man would prepare a meal since her own father only cooked on those rare occasions when her mother was away, and then they usually had TV dinners. "Do you know how to cook?" she asked.

"Of course," he answered. "Men in Hawaii always know how to make barbecues and that kind of thing. And in old Hawaii they did the cooking for everyone all the time."

"While you're cooking, Todd and I will go for a walk," Kai said, trying to sound as natural as he could. When Nathan looked at him in a surprised way, he added, "I want to look at my grandfather's property again."

"Go ahead, but be back in about twenty minutes," Nathan said as he and the girls climbed the stairs to the house.

CHAPTER XVII
At The Heiau

The boys followed the winding road and then a small trail deeper into the valley, the tall vegetation seeming to close in on them. They both hurried, knowing they had only a short time to find the *heiau*, hide the carving, and return to Nathan's before he got suspicious. They weren't sure exactly where the *heiau* was, except that Moana had said it was almost across from where they had buried the parrot.

Taking a side path, they found themselves amid towering bushes that Kai stomped through to look for the *heiau*'s ruins. One bush held a congregation of black carpenter bees that buzzed angrily when Kai stuck his face among them. Retreating quickly, the boys skirted a mud puddle and followed the path to its end where it rejoined the road again.

The next path disappeared into an overgrown thicket which Kai pushed his way through. In the distance was the sound of moving water, and he recalled Moana mentioning a stream near the *heiau*. Ducking under a tangle of branches, the boys emerged into a clearing. There beside the stream were the carefully piled stones that made up the temple.

Kai gazed with admiration at the *heiau* walls which looked as if they had been made last month instead of more than two hundred years before. It was in far better repair than the pile of overturned rocks that he had expected to find.

"Is this all there is?" Todd said, not knowing what a *heiau* should look like and feeling some disappointment at what he saw.

"What do you mean, is this all?" Kai felt the stirrings of anger at the other's insensitivity, then realized this was the first *heiau* that his friend had ever seen. "Yes, yes, this is all that's left now. . . the stone walls. This would have been the platform. On top there would have been buildings to store things, a tower for the priest to pray in, and statues of the gods. At least that's how it would have been at a big *heiau*. This is smaller so maybe people would have just left their offerings of fish and food on top, and there wouldn't have been any of those buildings."

He stepped closer to the rocks. "But we can't just leave the carving out in the open. Someone might come along and take it. We'll need to at least move some rocks and hide it underneath." He lay the carving on the platform and strode around the perimeter looking for a likely place to pull a few rocks loose.

Climbing onto the top, he struggled to remove several of the heavy stones. He paused and sat back to rest, "You know, it will just rot under the rocks. In the cave it was protected from the rain, but if we leave it here the rain will get to it and make it rot."

Worried that now Kai was making an excuse to keep the carving, Todd started to suggest that they find some plastic to wrap it in, but a noise from the underbrush silenced him.

"What are you two doing here?" Nathan said, stepping into the clearing.

Kai spoke first, managing to cover his surprise and guilt with a show of anger. "What are you doing following us?"

"I wasn't following you. I came to tell you to come back for lunch. Mother left some food, so I didn't need to cook. As I came along the road to get you, I saw you turn down this path. Now, you answer me. What are you doing here?" Nathan said.

Seeing the loosened rocks, he strode up to the *heiau*, an angry look on his face. "What have you done? Why are you moving these stones?"

As Nathan waited for an answer, Kai began to inch over to where the carving lay exposed.

Realizing that his friend was going to try and hide the statue, Todd made a quick decision. They needed an adult's help, and with Nathan's knowledge, he would be just the person to know what to do. Just as Kai was about to cover the carving, Todd jumped forward and grabbed it. "Kai found this in a cave on the mountain," he said. He waved the carving at the Hawaiian man and began a stream of stories about the burial cave, the missing adze, and the storm.

At first, Nathan understood very little of it, but as Todd talked he reached out and took the carving. He gasped when he saw the complete statue. "Did you find

this here at the *heiau*?" he asked.

"No," both boys answered at once.

Todd gestured in the direction of the distant mountain, excitedly repeating, "In the cave! In the cave!"

Seeing that Nathan still didn't understand, Kai took a breath and began the explanation. "Before you rescued me yesterday, I found a burial cave on Kualoa. The carving came from there."

"You're kidding," Nathan said.

"No, I'm not," Kai replied, and went on with the story of the missing adze and the storm. "Because of what happened to the boat, we were afraid that the statue was bringing us bad luck, so we were going to hide it here at the *heiau*," he concluded.

Nathan nodded his approval. "Yes, it's a good idea to bring it here, if you're sure that's what you want to do with it."

"Of course," Kai insisted. "After what happened I wouldn't dare keep it. And we knew Todd's parents wouldn't let us go back to the ranch, so we couldn't return it to the cave, even if that's the best place for it."

"I understand. Anyway, if you went back to that cave, neither of you is strong enough to pull the other up on the rope like I did," Nathan said.

"So you agree we have to put the carving back someplace safe?" Kai asked.

"Yes, I could never allow you to keep something like this. But maybe instead of hiding it away again, you should give it to the Bishop Museum. That place is full of ancient Hawaiian things like carvings. Of course you'd have to explain where you found it, and the scientists would want to go to the cave and look at the rest of the things, and maybe take them," Nathan said.

"I hadn't thought of that," Kai admitted, then shook his head. "The museum is a great place, but no, I don't think so. There were still bones in that cave, I don't want them disturbed. Everything should be left as it was."

"I'm glad you feel that way," Nathan said. "Nobody should take anything from burial caves, even scientists. Leave the old things where they belong, that's what people around here believe. In fact, I'd like to see that carving put back in the cave. But for now, set those stones back in place, and let's get back to the house for lunch. Bring the statue with you. I'll help you decide what to do with it."

CHAPTER XVIII
Nathan's Plan

By the time they had finished lunch, the boys had told the full story of the cave and the things they'd found there to their astonished sisters, whom Nathan insisted should know all about it.

"A tiki!" Moana exclaimed. She jumped out of her seat and almost tipped over the table when Kai pulled the carving out to show her and Julie.

"That's right. Though in Hawaii, statues like that were called *ki'i akua*," Nathan said, bending over to pick up the spoons and forks that Moana had knocked to the floor.

"Julie, you're not to tell Mom and Dad a word of this," Todd instructed his sister in a loud whisper. Seeing her skeptical look, he turned to Nathan for confirmation. "Isn't that right, Nathan? We shouldn't tell our parents, should we?"

"We'll see, but for now we'll keep it to ourselves," Nathan said.

Carrying the last of the dishes to the sink, he said, "I think we all agree that the carving should go back to the mountain. You boys said you wanted to return it there, and with my help, I think you can. Kualoa has always been a special place, and what came from there should go back to the same place. That way you can be sure no more harm will come to you, or to someone else who might accidentally find the carving."

Kai leaned forward with interest, "What do you mean Kualoa was special?"

"Goodness," Nathan sighed. "There are so many legends about that area that I can't remember them all. Probably it all comes from the early days when Hawaiians believed their gods were part of nature. Kualoa was supposed to be a form of one of the most important gods. That's never been forgotten."

"You sure know a lot about these things," Julie said with admiration.

"Well, I work at the ranch, so I hear things. Also, a couple years ago, I helped some university people who were doing research out there. Now that I think of it, there was a story about a burial cave that was supposed to be at Kualoa," Nathan said. He strode out of the room, and returned a moment later with a booklet that he thumbed through.

"Let me see. . ." he paused to find a particular passage. "Here it is, it mentions rumors of a burial cave for high chiefs. That must be it. It could be the cave you found."

"Wow! I knew there was something about that place when we saw lights there the first night," Kai let out a long breath.

To Nathan's questions about those lights, the boys recounted how they had seen torches spread out over the mountain the night the boat had rounded the point. "Kai thought they were nightmarchers," Todd concluded, glad to return to one of his favorite topics.

"Could be. I've never seen those lights, but there are plenty of stories of things like that. It wouldn't surprise me," Nathan said.

The five of them sat thinking of all that had been said. Nathan was the first to speak, "Maybe I should get a *kahuna* to bless this carving before we put it back. It has caused so much trouble, it might be a good idea."

"A *kahuna*?" Julie asked.

"That's like a priest for the Hawaiian religion," Moana explained.

"And they still have them?" Julie said.

"Oh, sure. At least I guess so, don't they, Nathan?" Moana said.

"Oh, my, yes." The man's chair creaked as he sat in it. "There's lots of people who call themselves *kahuna*, but we have to find one who can be trusted not to go telling this story to others, or to go up the mountain himself and disturb the cave. I think I know someone we can get."

"But how are we going to get over to the ranch to put the carving back without my parents getting suspicious? And tonight we have to go back to Uncle Bob's house since *Adventurer* is being towed away for repairs," Todd said.

"That is a problem. Anyway, it's too late today to be heading up that mountain, and that wouldn't leave time for the *kahuna*. Tomorrow would be better," Nathan said.

He rubbed his hand thoughtfully over his brow. "Why don't I invite all of you to spend the night here? After all, Kai and Moana are distant relatives, so that makes sense. We'll tell your parents that tomorrow we're going hiking or horseback riding. They shouldn't object as long as I'm along. When we've returned the carving, I can take you to your uncle's place."

"Are all of us going?" Julie asked, anxious to be included, although she knew almost nothing about riding horses. The only horses she'd ridden had been ponies at a carnival, and then she had been led around a ring on one.

"Sure, all of us will go," Nathan agreed, smiling at her.

"Great!" Kai said. Knowing that Nathan would help to return the carving made him feel as if a big weight had been lifted from his shoulders. He realized again how many things he needed to thank Nathan for.

CHAPTER XIX
The Kahuna

When the children and Nathan arrived back at the bay after lunch, *Adventurer*, although battered and beaten, was now upright and tied behind a powerful looking motor boat. Both boats lay floating in deeper water where *Adventurer* was waiting to be towed to Ala Wai Yacht Harbor for repairs.

After some hesitation, the Parksons gave permission for the youngsters to stay overnight with Nathan and Matilda. Several hours later, the youths and the Hawaiian man headed back into the now darkening valley.

"The house hasn't been this full since my brother came from California with his six children," Nathan said, as he switched the jeep's headlights on. "Mom will love it, and I have to admit that it does get pretty lonely up here."

The jeep rolled into the yard and pulled up to the house. Julie wasn't sure at first what seemed different, then realized it was the lights, or more accurately, the absence of electric lights. Instead of the harsh brightness of electricity, the home was lit by a soft glow. "Candles!" she said, thinking that it must have something to do with the *kahuna*, the mysterious priest, or whatever he was, who was supposed to come that night.

"Not candles, Julie," Matilda laughed as she greeted them. "It's kerosene lamps. We don't have electricity in this part of the valley."

With the help of the girls, Matilda soon had another big meal set out on the kitchen table: rice, sweet potatoes, fried fish that a neighbor had caught, and poi, a favorite dish of Hawaiians.

Julie dipped her fingers into the poi bowl, trying to get the hang of swirling the sticky substance around her fingers then flinging it into her mouth without dribbling it across the table or down her clothes. She wondered why the mashed taro root was among the favorite foods of Hawaiians. It seemed almost tasteless to her.

Nathan watched with an amused look as she made another attempt to get more into her mouth than she left in blobs on the table. "Glad to see you enjoying that," he said, mistaking her curiosity for approval. "Some people from the mainland say it tastes like library paste. Although, I've always wondered how they know what library paste tastes like. Anyway, we Hawaiians love our poi." He took another helping himself.

Matilda, her eyes on the boys, who had been quietly stuffing themselves, brought another platter of fish to the table. "Help yourself," she said, then called a welcome to a person she could see just outside the front screen door.

The door banged open, and a Hawaiian man about 40 years old entered. He was tall and vigorous looking, wearing a flannel shirt and work jeans. Sitting at a wooden bench, he began to pull his boots off.

"Hey, Kawika, these are some kids visiting us," Nathan said.

The stranger raised his hand toward them, "Glad to meet you." Having said that, he declined Nathan's invitation to join them for dinner, folded his hands in his lap, and shifted his gaze toward the ceiling, where it remained for the next twenty minutes while the others ate.

With dinner over, Matilda and the girls gathered up the dishes, while Nathan and the boys pulled up chairs beside Kawika. The man brought his attention back as if from some far away distance.

The two men talked a bit about things going on in the valley. Someone's taro patch that had been ravaged by pigs. . . a cow that had given birth. . . and the wells that the city wanted to drill to provide water for other parts of the island.

Their conversation droned on. Kai yawned. It was getting late. He wondered why the *kahuna* hadn't come, and he wanted to go to sleep. Just as it appeared that Nathan and Kawika might talk all night, they abruptly stopped.

"These are the boys I was telling you about," Nathan laid a hand on Kai's shoulder.

"I assumed as much. Which one of you found it?" Kawika said.

The boys looked questioningly at each other. "Found what?" Kai asked.

Kawika's head snapped back in surprise, there was a whistling sound as he took a breath of air through his mouth. "The burial cave. What do you think I came here for?"

Looking at the man more closely, Kai wondered if Kawika could be the *kahuna*. He had pictured a person in flowing white robes with a green maile lei around his neck, perhaps carrying a gourd or drum to beat out a chant, like the people you see leading hula groups. Instead, he had gotten Kawika, who was dressed like a farmer or cowboy.

"So who found it?" Kawika asked again, his eyes switching from boy to boy.

"I did. I'm the only one who went into the cave," Kai admitted.

Kawika's eyes seemed to bore in at him, and Kai shifted nervously in his seat.

"Here it is," Nathan said, distracting Kawika by handing him a cloth bundle that contained the carving.

"Nathan, the girls are bedded down in your room. I thought you and the boys could sleep out here," Matilda said, coming into the room. Pulling up a chair, she watched Kawika carefully remove the cloth that covered the carving. In the warm light of the kerosene lamp, the figure glowed with a reddish intensity.

"This is really something. I'm glad you boys want to put it back where it can rest with the spirits of the past," Kawika said. "Nathan asked me here to say a prayer over this and over all of you. Then this carving's spirit will know that in your hearts you have *aloha* for it and wish it no harm."

Opening a satchel that he had brought with him, he took out a dark wood bowl. It was cracked, but had been repaired in the old way by sewing the wood together. Into the bowl he poured some water from a plastic container. "Clean, fresh water from the mountain," he said, then pulled a bunch of ti leaves from the satchel.

He stood and said a prayer in Hawaiian. Taking one of the leaves, he dipped it into the bowl, withdrew it, and sprayed them all with droplets of water. Beads of moisture glistened on the carving. A stream of Hawaiian words followed, but neither Kai nor Todd could understand them.

As the prayer continued, Kai looked over at Matilda. She and Nathan sat in the same way, their eyes closed, and their hands folded in front of them. Kai could almost feel Kawika's warm breath touch him, and he dared a quick glance at the man.

The *kahuna* seemed to be in a trance, his eyes closed, the words flowing out, although his mouth barely moved. Even his voice seemed to have changed. It was at a higher pitch and sounded as if it came from a great distance. The room was filled with the sound of the *kahuna*'s prayer. For a moment, Kai thought he heard a drum beating, but a quick glance showed that no one was playing one.

The light in the room, already dim, seemed to grow more so. Glancing at Todd, Kai saw that his head was thrown back and that he was staring through unblinking eyes at the ceiling. Looking up, Kai saw only the metal rafters and roof. What could Todd be seeing? He looked again in case he had missed something, but it was just the same.

For a moment, Kai wondered if he were the only person in the room who was truly awake. Feeling alone, he glanced upward again. He felt as if he could see through the roof into the cloudless sky, where the stars burned brightly against the night's blackness.

He felt transported out of his chair and into the air. A refreshingly cool breeze blew against him. Alone, he seemed to be rushing upward, upward, into the heavens far above.

Like another part of his mind that he had never visited, he saw himself entering a cavern. It was cool, dark, and peaceful. There were carvings there, much like the one he had found, and he had the impression of other living beings. He couldn't see them, but he could feel them. A drum beat steadily in the background.

Then, almost as soon as it began, the dream, if that's what it was, ended. There was a flash of light. Kai shook himself, shivering, and looked at the others. They, too, were stirring back awake. Matilda smiled, Nathan stretched his arms, Todd shook himself. Wanting to say something, Kai started to, but realized he didn't know what words to use to describe what he had experienced.

Kawika looked at him with a smile. "That was good, you won't have any problems when you return the carving. It's ready to go back to where it belongs." The man stood up, folded the ti leaf, poured the leftover water into the plastic bottle, then slipped the wooden bowl into his satchel. He said, "Good night," and was at the door almost before Nathan had gotten to his feet to thank him.

The two men walked out to the yard while Matilda heaved herself up from the armchair and began arranging blankets on the floor. "You two sleep here," she said, indicating the simple beds, then lumbered down the hall to her own room.

"What did you think of that?" Kai asked, when he and Todd were alone.

"I don't know. I didn't understand most of it," Todd answered.

"Yeah, but what were you looking up at the roof for?" Kai asked.

"I don't remember. I think I fell asleep when Kawika said all those long prayers," Todd said. He yawned and stretched out on the blankets. Kai lay down beside him, wishing he had understood what had happened.

There was the sound of Nathan climbing the steps to the house. The kerosene lamp was blown out, and the man settled himself on the couch. Quiet fell over the home.

CHAPTER XX

Return To Kualoa

The next morning, just as the sun began to shine through the windows, Nathan woke the boys. "Let's get started," he said. When they had begun to stir, he went down the hall, knocked at the girls' door and gave them the same message.

A few minutes later they were all in the jeep on their way down the valley road. Out beyond the bay the sun was just peeking over the horizon. "What time is it?" Todd yawned. He always found it hard to wake up in the morning.

"About five thirty," Nathan said, then indicated a bundle of sliced bread and a jar of jam in a sack. "Help yourself. There's fruit juice in there, too."

A short ride brought them to the ranch which lay quiet in the early light. The air was still and only a few cows stirred, lazily munching on the long grass.

Disappearing into the stable, Nathan began to bring out horses and saddles. When the four friends had mounted, he pulled himself onto a black and white stallion and waved Kai and Todd to the lead.

They made their way to the other side of the

mountain and toward the far reaches of the valley. Julie tried to sit up straight and move lightly up and down in the saddle as she saw Moana doing. But her horse began to trot and she was afraid she might fall off. She tightened her grip on the reins, sat tightly in the saddle, and dug her legs into the mare's flanks.

Having Nathan behind her didn't help. She was sure he was watching her critically. When he asked several questions about her home in California, she didn't dare answer. It was taking all her concentration just to try and control the huge animal moving underneath her.

Finally it became clear that Rainbow, her mare with a mane that seemed to shimmer with many colors, knew more about what they were doing than she did, so she let the horse take the lead.

After several nervous minutes she began to feel more confident and allowed herself to look at the scenery around her. Ahead, at the far end of the valley, loomed a mountain with a sharp peak at the top. "We don't have to go up that, do we?" she asked Nathan.

"No, we're climbing Kualoa, this ridge here," he said, as he gestured at the towering mass to their side. Looking up its steep height, Julie felt no comfort in the thought of what lay ahead, and she began to wonder why she had wanted to come along.

Almost as if he'd read her thoughts, Nathan said, "You and Moana won't have to do any climbing. We'll leave the horses with you girls while we go up to the cave." He scanned the face of the ridge, looking for a sign of that cave, but from where they were he couldn't identify it for sure.

Ahead, Kai pulled his saddle bag toward him. For at least the fifth time he touched it to make sure the carving was inside where Nathan had put it. He knew it would be there, but still he was reassured when he felt it.

His thoughts raced ahead, and he imagined how it would be to put the carving back in the cave. They hadn't talked about it, but he knew he would have to be let down to the cave by a rope, the same way Nathan had rescued him.

Was there some way to get out of it? If he pretended he was sick, maybe Todd would volunteer to do the job. He glanced back at the others who followed. They seemed to be pushing him onward, as if they wouldn't accept any excuses. He gritted his teeth, straightened his shoulders, and breathed wearily. He felt like he was growing up.

When Kai reached the spot where he and Todd had left the horses tied the other day, he dismounted and waited for everyone else. Within a few minutes they were all ready. The girls had their instructions to watch the horses, Kai carried the carving in a backpack, Todd had a first aid kit, and Nathan hauled the rope.

With barely a good-bye to the girls, the three started along a path that threaded its way steeply up the mountain. They climbed quickly, familiar with where they wanted to go, and guided by the rock piles that Todd had left as markers.

Only once did they lose the trail, following the main path that turned and headed toward the back of the valley instead of continuing upward. Kai quickly realized they were going in the wrong direction and led them back to the cut-off they had missed.

A short while later, they were pulling themselves over steep rocks. Above them the mountain loomed, a gray cloud forming over its top.

Hauling himself up the incline, Kai realized they were off the trail again. Finding a level spot of ground, he set the pack down and sprawled to rest. As the others joined him, he recognized something familiar about the view. He got up and went to the edge where the ground was raw and broken from giving way recently. It was the spot from where he had fallen.

"Ah, here we are," Nathan said. The climb had tired him and he gasped for breath. "We came up a different way this time." He leaned over the ledge and checked that the tree was directly below so that Kai could grab it and pull himself toward the cave.

Leaning against a rock, Kai watched nervously as Nathan tied one end of the rope around a tree trunk. Before he could voice any doubts, Nathan had started to tie the free end of the rope around his waist.

"We'll do it this way so you have nothing to worry about," the man said. "You can't fall with the rope tied around you. Just hold on with your hands. That will keep you upright." He demonstrated how he wanted Kai to grasp the thick cord.

Kai managed to nod. His throat felt too dry to say anything, but there was plenty going through his mind. Falling over a cliff by accident, or hanging by a rope when you had to be rescued, was one thing. But doing it like this, because you had chosen to, seemed almost insane.

He stood as still as he could while Nathan fussed around, putting the backpack on him and pulling its straps tight under his arms and around his waist. "The carving is in the pack. When you get to the cave just put it back the way it was. And don't touch anything else," Nathan said.

"You don't really think I'd touch anything in that cave, do you? What, maybe you thought I'd take another statue?" Kai muttered.

Nathan smiled. "Glad to see you still have your sense of humor. Don't worry, brah, it will be easier this time. Your buddy and I will be holding onto the rope… we won't let anything happen to you."

In answer, Kai tightened the cord around his waist so he could feel it cut into his stomach. He wanted to know it was there, even when he wouldn't be able to see it. Then he edged forward. If he was going to have to drop over the edge, there was no point in waiting. He might as well get it over with.

"Just a minute," Nathan said, pulling him back. From the pack he took a small package wrapped in green ti leaf. "This is an offering. Kawika told me what to put in it, I made it this morning. It should quiet those spirits in the cave if they've been disturbed. Just put it in there when you leave the carving. OK, brah?"

Kai nodded and tried to flash a grin that he hoped looked confident and brave. He moved to the brink of the ledge where he kneeled and looked down. The valley seemed to spin far below. For a moment he felt dizzy and had trouble sorting out his thoughts. How was he supposed to drop over? Headfirst? He tried to pick through the alternatives. . . somehow headfirst did-n't seem like a good idea.

Then he felt Nathan beside him, gently turning him around, telling him how to let his legs slide over the ledge. "We'll let you down real slow. One more thing, this is a long rope. You don't have to worry about unty-ing it, just keep it around you when you go into the cave. We'll play it out little by little from up here."

Feeling the rope tighten around his waist, Kai watched Nathan brace himself. The man's feet were spread wide, the rope held tightly in his gloved hands.

Without allowing himself time to think what he was doing, Kai crawled backward. His legs dangled over the ledge. Then he was hanging by just one hand, the other firmly clutching the rope.

The earth began to crumble and he let go, falling straight down. He heard Nathan grunt as the rope cut tightly into his waist and he jerked to a stop. Little by little, he was let down. It was surprisingly easy. All he had to do was keep a grip on the cord. . .

CHAPTER XXI

Into The Cave

In a moment Kai had dropped to the level of the tree and reached out to its branches to pull himself toward the trunk. "I'm at the tree," he called excitedly. As more rope came down, it tangled in a long branch. Kai swung it loose, then dropped from the trunk to the spot of ground fronting the cave. Everything looked the same as it had before. "I'm going in," he called.

From above came a muffled reply that sounded like Todd saying, "OK."

Eager to finish his task, Kai climbed over the rocks and entered the cave, the rope trailing behind him. The darkness and damp, musty smell were familiar, and although he knew how to find his way, he felt more frightened than the first time. Now he knew this was a burial cave, he knew he shouldn't have taken anything from it, and he had seen what the angry spirits had done to the boat.

Edging cautiously forward into the cave, he tried to steady his shaking hands and knees. He was ready to flee if anything appeared threatening.

Feeling his way along the wall, he inched toward

the inner chamber. It seemed that just a few steps brought him to that familiar room, faintly lit by the crack that allowed light to enter.

At first glance, nothing appeared changed and Kai quickly swung his pack off and stepped toward the statues. He stumbled, but didn't fall. Kneeling among the ancient objects, he had the impression that he was being watched. He knew there was no one else there, but it was hard to shake the feeling that there was something.

He gazed up at a statue whose face was carved in a snarling grimace. He felt threatened, and he pulled at the pack's zipper to get the offering Nathan had given him. But his hands and arms felt as if they were asleep, and he could hardly lift them. His breath came in labored gasps. The air felt heavy, and he had to force his chest to expand so he could breathe.

The other carvings seemed to reach toward him. Two of the figures looked exactly like those in the vision he had when Kawika had been praying. Was this real, or had that been real? He felt confused, as if he might black out.

Summoning all his strength and concentration, he opened the pack and pulled out the ti leaf offering. He lay it in front of the statues. Then he took the small carving out, unwrapped it, and leaned it against the wall so that it was upright as it must once have been.

Breathing more easily, he stepped back. No longer did he have the feeling of being watched, or of being in danger. Perhaps the offering had done its work, or perhaps he had just imagined it all.

Taking a last look around, his eyes lingered on the small carving. It looked as he thought it should, and everything else appeared in order. He turned and slipped back into the darkness of the passageway.

CHAPTER XXII
Down The Mountain

Crawling through the cave's narrow opening and back onto the ledge, Kai stood and shielded his eyes from the bright sun. "I'm back," he called.

After a moment the extra rope began to be pulled upward in a slow, even manner until it yanked tight at his waist, then hauled him spinning toward the precipice. "Hey, wait a minute! I'm not in the tree yet." He gave the cord a sharp jerk.

The rope came slack in his hands, and he climbed onto the tree and into its outer branches. "Ready," he called.

With Nathan's first pull he was jerked free of the tree, swinging out over the valley amid a shower of broken branches. A moment later, he was pulled onto the ledge above.

Still holding tightly to the rope, he lay unmoving in the dirt until Todd grabbed him under the arms and yanked him away from the edge. Still not satisfied that he was safe, Kai crawled a few feet further toward the trail.

"Hey, come back here, or are you planning to go

down the mountain with that rope hanging from you?"
Nathan laughed.

Kai lay still as Nathan untied the rope. Finally free,
he stood up, surprised at how good he felt. "No problem. Everything is back the way it was," he announced.

"You left the offering there, too?" Nathan asked.

"Yeah," Kai nodded. A troubled expression crossed
his face as he remembered how the other carvings had
seemed to threaten him. It wasn't something he wanted to recall. Looking out on the peaceful valley, he
decided he would try to forget about this whole experience. He knew that he had gotten involved in things
that he should have left alone.

Nathan finished winding the rope and turned to
look at him. "You did a good job, brah. I guess that's it.
We're not leaving something behind?" He glanced at the
two for confirmation, then said, "Let's go then."

Todd led the way along the narrow path until it
joined the main trail where they began their slow
descent. They talked only a little, giving their complete
attention to the hazardous descent.

While the boys waited for Nathan to slide down off
a steep boulder, there was a sudden rumbling. Shielding
his eyes from the sun, Kai looked out to sea, searching
for a dark cloud that could cause the thunder he was
sure he'd heard. It had been so strong he'd even felt as
if it had shaken him.

He was excited at the possibility of one of the
island's rare electrical storms, but there was nothing
marring the blue sky except a thin, gray cloud over
Kualoa.

Then another rumbling. . . but this time so power-ful that it knocked both boys off their feet. Only Nathan remained upright as he spread his legs wide for bal-ance. Around them a few small rocks bounded off the mountain toward the valley below.

As the quaking subsided, the boys got up and dust-ed themselves off. "Wow, that was something!" Todd grinned, looking at Nathan for some kind of explana-tion. The worried look on the man's face stopped him from making a joke about what had happened.

Nathan was staring at the mountain towering over them, his mouth working as if he wanted to say some-thing.

"RUN!" he finally shouted. "*It's a landslide!* That was an earthquake and it's caused a landslide!"

Not quite sure where they should run to, the boys began to trot along a path that led toward the back of the valley. Over their shoulders they could see a cloud of dust that had covered the mountain top.

"Faster! Fast as you can! It's our only chance!" Nathan pushed at Kai as rocks tumbled past. There was a low rumble as the main body of falling rocks approached.

Sprinting as fast as they could, the boys dodged debris that landed on the narrow trail. Nathan's feet pounded behind them. Every few steps the man turned back to see which way the slide was advancing. If the whole mountain top had shaken loose, there would be no chance for them, but it looked like only the rocks near the burial cave had come free. If they could get far enough away from that area, they might be safe.

Small pebbles flew past them. One hit Kai underneath his right eye, and when he raised his hand to touch it, it came back spattered with blood. But he didn't stop running. The mass of rocks was now practically on top of them.

In the thick dust, Kai lost sight of the others. He felt a pressure on his back like that of a boulder that could crush him. He tried to outrun it, but couldn't. It pushed against him, pressing him to his knees, then to the ground and into the dust. Someone landed with a grunt beside him, and two hands pulled him forward.

Through the dust he could see Todd and Nathan kneeling beside him. They were all pressed against a stone ridge that reached up and out to create a shelf just above them. A surge of rocks struck against that lip of rock and bounced harmlessly around and off into the valley below.

After a few minutes the mountainside grew quiet as the slide passed. Only the dense dust hung in the air. The three waited under the ledge a while longer, then got to their feet, checking themselves for injuries. Except for Kai's cut cheek, which had stopped bleeding, no one had been hurt.

"I think it's safe now," Nathan said, peeking cautiously out from the protection of the ledge.

The boys nodded, too stunned to answer. Finally Kai said, "Some mountain! This place gives me the creeps."

They began to pick their way around the boulders and uprooted bushes. In the tumult of rocks, the path had been swept away. They would have to find their own way to the valley floor.

While Todd followed the others, he saw where the rocks had come to rest below, and he immediately thought of Julie and Moana.

"The girls and the horses were there!" he yelled. His voice broke as he pointed ahead to a mound of debris that lay over what had been trees and bushes.

The climbers came to a halt, searching for a sign of the girls. . . but everything living seemed to have been swept away.

"This darn mountain!" Nathan shook his fist angrily. He looked up as if waiting for a reply, but except for the wind that whistled past, there was silence.

After a moment they turned back to continue their descent, quickening their pace as much as safety would allow.

CHAPTER XXIII
Reunited

Out on the valley floor, Moana and Julie tried to calm their fear-crazed horse. Moments earlier, when the earth had trembled, the girls had looked up to see a cloud of dust surrounding Kualoa's summit. When the crescendo of falling rock had reached their ears, Moana, realizing what was happening, had loosened the ropes that restrained the horses. She had whipped all but one of them, sending them fleeing toward the other side of the valley and safety.

The girls had tried to mount the remaining horse, but he had sensed the danger and was jumping wildly. It was all they could do to hang on to the reins as the horse dragged them out onto the valley floor where they were safe from the landslide.

Now, as the dust settled, they tried to calm the horse so Moana could ride for help. One look at the scar of rocks on the mountainside, and it was clear that the boys and Nathan would need help.

"Whoa, boy," Moana said as calmly as she could, stroking the horse's muzzle. Julie also added soothing words, trying not to think that her brother might be buried under the landslide.

After the shattering movement of rocks and the shaking of the earth, it seemed strangely quiet. In that silence, Julie believed she heard someone call her name, but thought it must be their own voices echoing among the nearby boulders. She glanced around just to be sure.

Turning back to the horse, something caught her eye. For an anxious moment she held her breath until she was sure.

"Nathan! Nathan!" she cried. She and Moana ran toward the man who was so covered with dust that it was hard to pick him out from the surrounding stones. Before they reached him, Kai and Todd appeared over the rocks and began to make their way over the last few feet to the floor of the valley.

Reunited with their brothers, Julie and Moana threw their arms around the boys and then around Nathan. It was hard to tell who was most excited.

"My gosh! How did you survive?" Julie asked.

In the babble of conversation that followed, they traded stories of what each had done when the landslide sent them all scrambling for safety.

"At least that carving is back in the cave," Kai said as they walked toward the highway and back to the ranch house. He looked up at the changed appearance of the mountain. "We'd never be able to find the entrance to the cave now."

"You're right, son," Nathan agreed. "That whole part of the mountain has been swept away and covered with new rock. It seems kind of strange that it happened only where the cave is, and just after we put the carving back. Look up there. I don't see rock slides anywhere else. Only near the cave."

The friends nodded. Nathan was right, there was no sign of damage or change anywhere else.

"What's it mean?" Kai asked.

"Oh, I don't know. It's one of those things you can't explain. But the coincidence is a bit too close for me. Maybe it's meant for no one else to ever find that cave," Nathan said.

They went on in silence, thinking about Nathan's idea. Todd accepted it was true. No longer would he say that Hawaii's gods and their powers didn't exist. He had been touched by them, and he would never be the same again. He wasn't just a stranger now, a *haole* from someplace far away. After what he had seen and experienced, he had become a child of the land.

Along the dusty road leading to the ranch house, a jeep bumped toward them. It slowed, and the smiling, brown face of one of the ranch workers leaned out. "Nathan, you buggah, what you doing with these kids walking around on such a hot day? You all look like you been swimming in dust."

Nathan grunted, saying, "The other horses got loose in that big earthquake."

The driver's smile grew a bit wider as if expecting there was going to be a funny punch line to the story. "What earthquake dat?" he asked.

"You mean you didn't feel an earthquake?" Nathan asked and shook his head, unable to believe it.

"I been here all morning, bruddah, nothing happen here," the man said.

"Look, there at the rock slide," Nathan pointed to the mountain with its fresh scar from the recent landslide.

"Holy cow!" The driver's mouth dropped open to its fullest extent. "And we didn't feel a thing in da ranch house!"

Leaving the man staring at the mountain, the five continued along the road. "Well, I guess that clinches it," Nathan said. "Any regular earthquake that could shake loose so much stone would have been felt all over this side of the island. If we're the only people who felt it, then that was no regular quake. No, that mountain covered up the burial cave on purpose. It didn't want anyone else going in there, and we better leave it that way. None of us should tell anyone else about that cave. *Ever.*"

The four friends quickly nodded their agreement.

CHAPTER XXIV
Three Weeks Later

A strong wind blew a spray of salt water over the boys as they leaned out from the bow of the newly repaired *Adventurer*. In the early light of dawn, they could see clouds low on the horizon ahead. Under those clouds lay the island of Kaua'i.

Little more than an hour later, *Adventurer* had reached the rugged, mountainous shoreline of Kaua'i and was coasting along the remote Na Pali Coast. Kai wiped the spray from his face and followed Todd to the stern deck where they joined their sisters and Mr. and Mrs. Parkson.

"We finally made it to Kaua'i! Three weeks late, but no harm done," Mr. Parkson said.

"*Adventurer* is sailing well," Mrs. Parkson agreed. "I was a little worried that those repairs might have changed it in some way, but it's like the same old *Adventurer*."

Julie set aside the diary she'd been writing in. "It is the same, Mommy. It just has a different mast, and new paint."

"And a new cabin roof," Moana reminded her friend.

"And new furnishings," Mrs. Parkson added amid laughter.

While the adults reminisced about how the water spout had damaged *Adventurer*, the four friends looked silently at each other. They had never shared their own belief that the storm had been caused by the ancient Hawaiian gods. Nor would they probably ever be able to tell the adults about the landslide that had nearly killed them, since they would also have to tell them about the burial cave.

Quiet fell over all the travelers as they sailed into the shadows cast by high mountains rearing straight up from the sea. The sails flapped loosely as the wind was cut off by nearby land.

Mrs. Parkson shivered. The air was chilly in the shadows where the sun hadn't yet reached. She wasn't sure if she liked the gloomy, deserted feel to this coast. Looking up at the rugged mountains where there was no sign of human life, she saw waterfalls, too numerous to count, that fell hundreds of feet down steep mountainsides. A broad valley they were sailing past also seemed untouched by humans. It was choked with trees in all shades of green, and flowers of outrageous colors.

"I wish we could go into that valley," Julie said, dreaming of staying in a grass shack, swimming in tropical pools, and decorating herself with leis of sweet smelling flowers.

"It's almost impossible to get into these valleys, isn't it?" Mr. Parkson asked Kai. He repeated the question when Kai didn't respond.

Suddenly realizing that everyone was looking at him, Kai dropped the binoculars he'd been using to inspect the mountains. He was sure he had seen caves high up on the valley wall, and he was wondering what they might contain.

In the last three weeks he had begun to think of himself as something of a scholar on caves. He had read several books on life in old Hawaii, especially the parts on burial caves. With Todd, he had made two trips to the Bishop Museum to study their collection of carvings and other remains of ancient Hawaiian life.

To Mr. Parkson's repeated question, he answered, "That's right. It's hard to travel along the Na Pali coast except by boat. If you hike in, the trail is very rugged. Not many people do it."

The boat began to slip past the valley, and Kai handed the binoculars to Todd. "Look up there. I'm sure I saw a cave. It wasn't just dark shadows. You can actually see where the cave opens up."

Todd thrust the binoculars back at Kai. "I'm not interested in any more caves. And you're not going into any on this trip either. Remember what happened last time."

"I don't want to explore it. I was just pointing it out," Kai said. As he made his way forward to the boat's bow, Todd followed him.

Leaning against the cabin roof, Kai trained the binoculars on the high cliffs. Some of the dark spots seemed to be only shadows, while others definitely looked like caves. They might not be burial caves, but he knew from his research that this inaccessible region would have been just what Hawaiians looked for when it came time to bury the bones of dead chiefs. They had wanted places that would be very hard for anyone else to ever find.

"There's another one!" He tapped his friend on the arm and pointed out a spot that seemed to lead to a shadowed interior. But before Todd could decide whether or not to look, the boat slipped around the cliff and left the lonesome valley and caves behind.

In a little while, they entered busy Hanalei Bay. Making their way past water skiers towed by buzzing motorboats, they dropped anchor in clear turquoise water near a cluster of sailboats.

Ahead lay a large valley looking like a giant checkerboard in various shades of green where different crops were being tended. On a far bluff a hotel overlooked the bay, while another hill was covered with houses that seemed as small as matchboxes.

Kai snapped the binoculars shut. "We're back to civilization. No more secret caves, I guess."

He sounded disappointed as he looked back toward the rugged coast they had just sailed past. "But I know I could find something back there if I had the time to look," he said.

Pau